PRISCILLA

PRISCILLA

By COLENE COPELAND
Illustrated By EDITH HARRISON

JORDAN VALLEY HERITAGE HOUSE

Library of Congress Catalog
Card number: 81-80663

ISBN: 0-939810-01-8 (Hardcover)
ISBN: 0-939810-02-6 (Softcover)

Second Printing

To my loving husband Bob,
who willingly shared our home and our vacation
with a special little pig.

AUTHOR'S NOTE

Priscilla was a real live pig ----not a figment of my imagination. In fact, all of the animals named in this book were real.

Although Priscilla adds a little color now and then in the telling, the "events" in the story actually took place.

CONTENTS

PRISCILLA

Chapter 1

TOO BIG FOR THE HOUSE

MAMA had always let me sit on her lap to watch television. How was I to know that one day she would say, "Priscilla! You are *too* heavy for me to hold." She picked me up and gently tucked me in, by her side, on the couch.

Mama looked uneasy. "The time has come to move you out to the barn," she said.

The barn? How could she suggest such a thing? What do I know about living in a barn? *Nothing!* That's what.

Papa looked amused, "Who's going to teach her to act like a pig?" he asked.

"My Priscilla is *very* bright. She'll learn," Mama answered. "I hate to see her grow up. She's the cleanest pet I've ever had in the house. Wish there was some shot we could give her to keep her from getting any bigger."

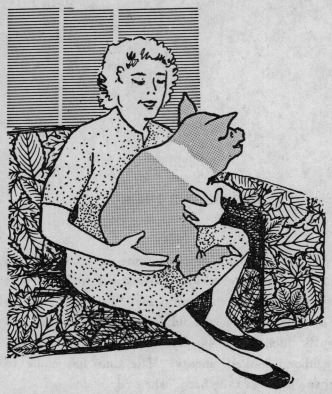

"But there isn't," Papa said. He picked me up and put me on his lap. "She knows people, Mama. But this kindhearted little thing wouldn't last ten minutes with a batch of hogs. She's strong enough now, but she's pure pet."

"That's right, dear. We must be careful how we handle her transition from the house to the barn," Mama said. "I wouldn't have her hurt for the world."

Papa's question bothered me. "Who is going to teach her to act like a pig?" he had said. I wonder what he meant by that. It's not my fault if I don't act like a pig. If anyone is to blame it should be an old sow named Mabel, my real mother. *Some mother* she is! Doesn't even like me. My own mother! She laid all five hundred pounds of herself on me the day I was two days old! Lucky for me Papa and Mama were near and heard me squealing. They got there just in time. Papa poked Mabel real hard, trying to get her up off of me. She finally raised one shoulder. Mama lifted me out, thinking I was dead. I *nearly* was.

They took me to the house. I don't remember the first few days, but I know Mama took care of me. I drank milk from a baby's bottle and slept on the bed with my new parents. Mama's poodle, Mitzi, "housebroke" me. I noticed she scratched on the back door when she wanted out. So, I did it too. I even went to California in the car with Mama and Papa, on vacation. I'll tell you more about that later.

When I was feeling better, Mama tried to give me back to my mother, but she wouldn't take me back. She pushed me away. Mabel didn't want to be bothered with me. Makes me sad to think about it. Sometimes, it makes me mad!

Papa's eyes were closed and his head was tilted back against his chair. I think he was worried about me too. "Mama, do you think Priscilla understands what we're saying?"

"Of course. Every word," she answered.

"You're awfully sure of yourself," Papa chuckled.

"I *am* sure," Mama told him. "Remember the day we brought her in from Mabel's pen?"

"I remember," he answered drowsily.

"Right away, I named her 'Priscilla'. The name fits her perfectly. I told her we love her and would not let her die. She understood. She *still* understands. -----every word." Mama was positive.

"If you say so, Mama," Papa said. He was not convinced.

All I could think about was getting moved out. I would be put in a pig pen, no doubt. What will it be like? Papa said I wouldn't last ten minutes with a batch of hogs. Maybe I'll be *killed* right away! Golly! I don't want to think about it.

But Mama said she wouldn't have me hurt for the world. So, I guess I'll just have to wait and see.

Sometimes, when Papa and Mama go out to feed the hogs and clean the pens, my friend Mitzi and I go along. I like that. We run around in the back of the station wagon. Once in a while Mitzi gets to bark at dogs in other cars, but I never, ever, see another pig in a car.

When our Oregon weather is agreeable Mitzi and I play outside. We race around the barns. She sniffs and smells everything. I root up the ground. I don't know why I root up the ground. It just seems like the thing to do.

We love to pester the nanny goats. They get mad and stomp their feet and give us dirty looks.

The chickens outsmart us. When they see us coming they fly up in the trees. That really aggravates Mitzi. She doesn't like to be outdone by a chicken.

One day I peeked inside the farrowing barn, the place where big sows go when they are about ready to have their babies, or whenever they are looking for a husband. What a racket! There were noisy, ill-mannered sounds of eating. Someone was *slurping* water.

Papa had been hauling cedar shavings in the old red wheelbarrow. Just as I was about to go in, so was he.

"Come on in, Priscilla," he invited. "Look the place over. You will be spending time in this barn, someday."

I stood in the wide doorway. I could hear little pigs' voices, but I couldn't see them.

There was one big sow in each of the pens. Some of them stared at me. One yelled!

"Hey, pig! Why aren't you in the feeder building?" she croaked, in an unladylike voice. I was too frightened to answer.

"You there, pig," she shouted, "I'm *talking* to you. Can't you hear?" No one had ever spoken to me so cruelly before.

Finally, I mustered up enough nerve to say, "I don't live in the feeder barn. I live in the house with Mama and Papa." I turned my eyes away from her cold unfriendly stare and looked for Papa.

"What! ——*You live where, with who?"* she mocked.

"I live in the house with Mama and Papa," I repeated shyly.

She began to laugh fiendishly. The others joined her. They all turned their attention to me and shouted loud, cold-hearted remarks. Someone called me "Little Miss Super Pet". Another one said, "The dumb little creep doesn't know she's a pig."

I couldn't see anything funny to laugh about. I began to cry.

Mitzi heard the commotion. She saw my predicament. "Don't pay any attention to those ugly old hogs, Priscilla. They are *jealous* of you. Come on," she coaxed. "Let's go for a run in the orchard."

"You go ahead," I blubbered. Tears were streaming down my face. I hurried around to the side of the barn, out of sight. I could still hear them laughing. I felt terrible.

Never, will I forget *that* day. How can I make Mama and Papa understand? Hogs don't like me!

Chapter 2.

A NEW HOME FOR ME

THAT night I slept a restless sleep. I dreamed terrible, frightening dreams! Seven monstrous black sows attacked me! They snapped me up with their tough snouts and tossed me about like a Kansas cyclone! I wiggled and jerked and managed to escape! But as soon as I was free from them an army of scarlet, long tusked boars, charged me from every direction! They were blood thirsty! There was no escape! I was doomed to suffer their torture! They pinched, bit, slapped and shook me! They knocked me down, kicked me and spit on me! All the while they laughed a gory laugh. I suffered great pain! They seemed to relish my agony.

Mama was in my dream. I could hear her voice but I could not see her. "Pris---cil---la," she called to me.

My enemies continued to tear at my flesh!

8

Mama's voice grew nearer. Finally, I saw her running toward me. A thick grey mist boiled up all around her. She could not reach me.

Suddenly, a great white sow came charging through the mist! Her unexpected presence startled my abductors! She rushed toward me gently lifting me on her strong nose. She tossed me to Mama. I knew I was safe----at last.

What a nightmare! I tried to wake up. I was crying so hard my head ached. My heart was pounding so fast I bounced off my pillow. I tumbled to and fro. My head banged against the bedroom wall. *That* woke me up.

My pillow was wet with tears.

Slowly, I stood up on rubbery legs and checked my body for scars. How lucky for me to survive such an ordeal. I thought of the beautiful white sow who had saved me from utter destruction.

I chose to stay awake for the rest of the night. Going back to bed could mean having another of those *awful* dreams. I certainly couldn't risk having *that* happen!

Slipping quietly out of the bedroom I headed for the living room. I flipped on the television with my nose and jumped up on the sofa. A young man in a red checked shirt was giving the early morning farm report. I was in no mood to hear about the price of hogs. So, I crawled in under an oversized sofa pillow until some music came on.

Before long the little gold alarm clock by the bed began to ring. Quickly, I turned off the T.V., dashed to the bedroom and jumped on my pillow. No need to worry Mama and Papa about my restless night. I did not want to be troublesome.

Mitzi bounced around on the bed, waking up Mama and Papa. She looked silly. Mitzi sleeps between the pillows on the bed. I *used* to sleep there, when I was smaller. Lately, my bed has been a big soft pillow on the floor, on Mama's side of the bed.

Frequently, in the night, when I get scared or lonesome, I hop up on the bed and snuggle up between Papa and Mama. Papa grumbles about it, but Mama just scratches my ears and says, "Go back to sleep, Priscilla." So I do.

Mitzi ran straight for the kitchen door, barking. Papa let us out. We darted to the back yard.

Even though the grass was wet, this was my favorite time to be in the back yard. The skinny lady next door would still be sleeping. She often peeks over the fence at us and gives us dirty looks.

Mitzi and I checked out the entire back yard to see if any dogs had paid us a visit during the night. None had. A spotted frog hopped along under the lilac bush. An Oregon bluejay sat on a fence post and squawked. He thinks he owns the back yard. But Mitzi and I know better.

A couple of walnuts were lying on the ground. Just as I was about to sink my teeth into one, Mama called, "Breakfast is ready!" *Scrud!* I *wanted* those nuts!

We raced to the house! Mitzi let me win today. Mama held the door open and laughed when I wiped my feet on the mat.

"You are the cleanest pet I've ever had in the house, Priscilla," she said with a smile in her voice. I've heard her say that before. It must be a fact.

"I'll bet we're the only people in the world who own a pig who lives in the house and wipes its feet on the mat to boot," Papa chuckled.

I like it when they say nice things about me. Mitzi would get bragged on too if she would wipe her feet on the mat. But she just stands there until Mama wipes the morning dew from her feet, with a rag.

Breakfast was delicious. I had a bottle of warm milk, plus--- Mitzi's leftovers.

I listened to every word that was said at breakfast. I sort of hung around under the table. Crumbs drop on the floor sometimes. But with me around they never know it.

"Priscilla has to be with her own kind," Mama said. "I hate to put her out! Is there no other way, dear?"

"We have no right to keep her from a normal life! Someday she will want pigs of her own. Right now --- she's so tame! It will be easier if she can make the adjustment now while she's young," he answered.

Babies of my *own?* Gee! I had never thought about being a ----mother!

Doomsday arrived! I was whisked away to the station wagon. Mama was crying. I felt awful. Nobody said a word while Papa drove the three miles to the hog barns. I didn't feel like looking out the windows or running around in the back. I settled for a spot on the front seat and kept quiet.

The road became bumpy. Gravel peppered the bottom of the car. I knew without looking we had arrived at the farm.

The hogs shouted the news of our coming to each other. Papa's arrival meant breakfast would soon be served. I'll bet they wouldn't be so anxious if they knew that I was moving in!

Curiosity overtook me. I gathered my courage and took a peek out the window. Papa drove past the farrowing barn. Boy! What a relief! He breezed by two more buildings and then another. *Where* are they taking me?

We moved on, through the old orchard. Two nanny goats stood still and followed us with their eyes. We passed the empty sheep shed. Papa doesn't like sheep all that much.

Finally! We came to a stop by the lofty, newly restored machine shed. The old roof had been re-placed. Walls that were once windowless boasted shiny clean panes.

Mitzi and I had checked this building out plenty of times. Except for Papa's tractor, it's empty.

There was a fenced yard in the front of the shed, a nice addition! The fence was put together in sections of unpainted wood. Each section was attached to small square posts which had been set in the ground. A bright green gate led us into the yard.

Papa directed us to a sliding door cut in the front of the shed. He gave it a saucy little shove to the right. The door flew open. And, *there it was!* A brand new pen. Entirely unused. Wasn't hard to guess who it was built for!

The pen was much larger than those in the far-rowing barn. Yet, it sort of got lost in such an over-grown building. The little pen looked ----lonely.

I had no idea it would be so *private* and ----safe.

"Look it over, Priscilla," Mama said. "It's all yours."

So *this* is where I'll be living, not with other hogs,

but *here*, by myself, away from everybody. How strange! Hadn't Mama said I should be with my own kind? Am I the *only one* of my kind? Are there no others like me? Am I to be *alone, forever?* How could they do this to me?

I looked at my "parents" and fought back the tears. I would *not* cry. I did not want to be troublesome. After all, hadn't they built this pen especially for me. It *was* nice, *really* nice.

The floor was made of smooth wood and covered with fresh, sweet smelling cedar shavings. Once, I saw a dance floor on television, just like this. The floor looked inviting. I ran a few feet and put on my brakes. Wow! Did I go sliding. I did it again and again. Shavings flew every which way! It was fun. I was having a good time.

Suddenly, I spied the inviting pile of golden wheat straw that lay in one corner. I jumped right in, crawled underneath and ran out the other side with pieces of straw on my head. Mitzi would love this place, I thought.

Papa and Mama laughed at my buffoonery. They like seeing me happy.

"I think she likes this place," Papa said. "Let's leave her be for now. We're late with the chores."

I could see it pained Mama to leave me. She kept looking back as they left the building.

Maybe it won't be so bad here, I thought.

As soon as I was alone I began to snoop. First I checked out my yard. There was a sunken grassy spot. I didn't like it until I discovered how well my body fit into it, a perfect spot for sun bathing.

There was a new metal oil drip pan filled with fresh drinking water. It won't be the same as home! At home, Mitzi had a water dish. When no one was looking, I'd take a sip. Water always tasted better to me from a baby's bottle. It had its benefits. I got more attention with the bottle, also back rubs and conversation. *Now*, when I'm thirsty, I'll have to drink from this old pan.

There were two doors on my pen, the sliding door that leads to the yard and a swinging gate that opens up to the inside of the machine shed. Inside, by the gate, sat a wooden "V" shaped box. There was nothing in it. Perhaps it's a waste paper basket. I'll have to ask Mama.

The pen was nice and neat when we arrived. But not now! I had really messed up the place. The floor, once evenly covered with cedar shavings, had ugly looking bare streaks where I had slid. My straw was scattered like confetti after a New Year's eve party. I saw that on television too, in a late late movie. Suspecting the straw was my bed, common sense told me if I wanted a nice place to sleep I'd better clean house. And, I wanted Mama to be proud of me.

I rooted around in the shavings until the floor

looked presentable. With a little fluffing up, the straw proved to be quite comfortable. It was different than my pillow behind the bed, much different. But then, those comforts are gone ----gone forever.

As I lay there in wonderment, I had a most peculiar feeling, a very strange sensation, as if I were being watched. No one was in sight. I could see the nannies in the orchard and a few chickens pecked around the exposed roots of a knobby tree, but *they* weren't looking my way.

Who would want to look at me? No one will ever care for me except Mama and Papa. I'll be lonesome here.

Mama returned carrying a bucket. She poured something that looked like cereal in the "V" shaped box.

"Come on, Priscilla," she said. "I want you to try some of these pig pellets. They're made of corn and alfalfa and lots of other good stuff to help you grow. The other pigs eat them and like them a lot. Come and try some."

Well now! Let's see what pigs eat. I got up and looked at it. It smelled like bread, but it was crunchy little pieces. I tried a couple. They were o.k. but I wasn't hungry. Besides. there was that feeling again that someone was watching me, and it wasn't Mama.

I felt silly as I glanced about. I was scared! Maybe I should tell Mama! Maybe not. I'd be embarrassed.

"You're going to be o.k., Priscilla," Mama assured me. "I'll be back after a bit." She patted me on the head and noticed how clean my place was. "No one would *ever* believe how you've straightened this place up. You are something else, Priscilla!" She left.

"But Mama," I said, after she had gone, "I'll be lonesome here." I began to cry.

Chapter 3.

T.C.

I cocked my head and strained to follow the sound of the station wagon as it rumbled softly away on the bumpy gravel road. Then for a long while, I pondered my situation. One of a kind! That's me! I fall far short of being *in the know* when it comes to *pig know how,* can *scarcely* be called a *person,* knowing full well I act like one. Yet, here I am, isolated from pigs and people and the whole wide world. I'm all alone, and yet, there is that constant feeling of being watched! Maybe it's God! Hadn't Mama said that God would watch over me?

Suddenly, a husky voice burst forth from the sky. "Been moved out, huh?"

"Wha----?" I whirled around! Cedar shavings flew every which way! *Seeing* nothing, I dived into my straw pile and hid! Only my tail stuck out. I was so frightened my body shook all over, causing the entire

18

straw stack to quiver!

The voice laughed. It *sounded* friendly.

Slowly, I stuck my head out to have a look. But I still didn't see anyone.

I came right to the point. "Are you God?"

The voice laughed again. "Mercy no! But I do know a lot of females who sort of glorify me. Some think me to be quite princely. Sort of a Prince Charming, maybe. But, sacred, Lordly? -----I kinda doubt it."

"Where are you please?" I asked politely thinking it might be God ----teasing me.

"Up here. In the tractor seat," it said.

I looked up. There he sat, in Papa's big tractor seat, grinning down at me.

"You're not God! You're a cat!" I said, a little disappointed.

"Oh! I've always known that. *You* are the one who thought I was God," he answered as he raised up and flexed his muscles. "I kinda liked it, you thinking I was God. It had a nice ring to it."

It was plain to see this cat lacked humility! He *really* liked himself a lot. But he *was* friendly and it would be wonderful to have a friend.

"You really *scared* me, cat!" I scolded. "I don't think it's nice to spy on people! You *have* been watching me. Haven't you?"

"Sure have," he answered shamelessly. "There's

not much excitment around here. A guy can get pretty bored, even a little lonesome."

"You? Lonesome?" I asked, *very* surprised. How could a character like this tom cat ever find time to be lonesome? Perhaps he was just trying to make me feel good.

"Sure! I'm normal you know. Well ----almost, anyway," he laughed. "Lately I've been watching 'em put up this new home of yours. Pretty fancy pad for a porker! Do you know you're the only pig on the place with private living quarters? Not to mention your own fenced yard."

"Honest? I am?"

"Betcha didn't know you were *that* special," he said as he began his descent from the tractor seat landing on the top boards of my pen. How graceful he is! As well as being the most handsome he was by far the largest cat I had ever seen. Of course, I haven't seen very many.

His coat was short but not harsh. There were black pencilled markings to the head, forming an "M" on the face. More swirls were on his cheeks, rings around the eyes and chest and more dark swirls and stripes here and there over the rest of him. I could see greys and white underneath a lot of black tips. He looked a lot like Tiger, the tabby who lives in the house, except for size. He was well proportioned, for a cat. But I dare not tell him for fear he would become more vain than ever.

His majesty settled himself on a corner post of my pen and peered down upon me through large round eyes.

To think, I had actually mistaken this cat, for God! The best I could hope for was that God was busy with someone else and had not noticed how I had made a fool of myself.

If God was listening to either of us it was probably the cat. Why? Because the cat liked being called God. He said it had a nice ring to it.

But there he sat, smiling. What do you say to a guy like this?

"Do you know all the other pigs?" I asked.

"Certainly," he answered.

"I've never been around any other pigs. I've lived in the house with Mama and Papa since I was just two days old," I said.

"I know all that," the cat told me. "By the way, they call me T.C. ---That's short for Tom Cat."

"Pleased to meet you," I said. "I am called Priscilla. Priscilla isn't short for anything, but Mama told me once that my name comes from the Roman word, Priscus. Priscus means *former*."

"Oh! That's nice," he said. "-------I think." We both laughed a little. I was having a real good time.

"I was ---wondering. Do you think we can be friends?" I asked shyly.

"Sure kid! Why not? A guy can't have too many friends. When I saw you down here in your pen all alone and feeling sorry for yourself, I said to myself, 'Self, be a good scout and go down there. Be a friend to that lonely little porker.' So, knowing good and well that I give good advice, I took it." The Tom Cat was playing my big brother. I liked it.

He continued. "We've all known for a long time that the Mr. and Mrs. wouldn't keep you away from your own kind much longer. In fact, I've been taking all bets that you would be here today."

"You have? The Mr. and Mrs.? Is that what you call Mama and Papa?" I asked eagerly.

"Everybody but you, Priscilla," he laughed.

"So what? They will always be Mama and Papa to me. And, you shouldn't bet. It isn't nice," I scolded.

"It is when you've got a cinch bet. My brother, Tiger. He gave me the exact date."

"Tiger, is your brother?" I was surprised!

"Yep, but we have different fathers," he grinned. His remark made me blush.

That conniving scoundrel. How clever he is. With the exact date of my arrival from Tiger, he did have a cinch bet!

Although T.C. was the only friend I had around at the present, I didn't want him to think *he* was the only friend I had. I told him that Tiger was a friend of mine, also Mitzi and Cleo. The fact that Cleo was only a baby chicken was information I did not care to share. For now, at least, I chose not to mention it.

"By the way, Tom Cat, how come I haven't seen you around here before?" I asked.

"Well I've seen *you* enough times running in and out of buildings and rooting up grass in the orchard. Problem is, you're always with that dog. Me and the mutts don't hit it off. Never did. When I spy one in my domain I climb a tree and hope it gets bitten by a billy goat. ---Barking bugs me." T.C. was serious.

I was shocked to hear that Mitzi was his enemy. She is my best friend. Tiger and Mitzi get along fine. It was hard for me to understand T.C.'s feelings. In the house everybody got along together. Lots of times Mitzi, Tiger, Cleo and I all crawled into the same box in the house and took naps, because we ----- loved each other.

"Do other cats like you?" I asked.

"That's a *dumb* question. *Of course* other cats like me. Why shouldn't they?" He was disturbed by the idea that anyone would dislike him.

"I don't think the other pigs will like me!" I said, revealing my greatest fear and feeling once again like crying.

T.C. quickly assured me that other pigs *will* like me. But I was not so sure. I could not forget the day I followed Papa into the farrowing barn and how those big sows made fun of me. I thought of my dream and the hogs who tried to kill me.

When bed time came I missed Mama and Papa and Mitzi. I missed my bottle of warm milk. It was hard to be brave but I knew I must try to act like a pig, although I wasn't too sure how a pig acts. I did not want to be troublesome.

T.C. was over in a far corner of the machine shed eating a mouse. It looked terrible! What a mess! How could *anybody* eat a mouse?

I mosied over and tried to eat some pellets, but I had no appetite. If I couldn't eat maybe I could sleep. I fluffed up my straw and lay down. I couldn't sleep either. I wanted to go home. Why did I have to get too big for the house? Would I ever see another pig? I was *so* lonely.

Chapter 4.

GETTING A SECRET TREAT

A car pulled up. It was Mama and Papa and Mitzi. T.C. leaped up to the rafters and looked down. I was anxious to tell them about my new friend.

"You're not eating your food, Priscilla!" Papa sounded aggravated. I'll have to try harder, I thought, not wanting to be troublesome. I dashed right over to my feed box and gulped down a few pellets.

"We'll just have to wait and see," Mama said.

"Wait and see for what?" Papa asked.

"To see if she *will* eat and adjust to this pig pen." Mama answered. She sank down on my straw. I ran over and jumped in her lap and very quickly got shoved off.

"Priscilla," she yelled, "you can't do that anymore. You're just too darned heavy."

She scared me! I plunged for the far side of the

26

pen. Mama was laughing.

"I didn't mean to scare you, Darling," she said playfully. "Come here --lie beside me --put your head in my lap."

I accepted the invitation. Turned out to be o.k. for me. Mama rubbed my back and said, "God loves you, my Priscilla. He will watch over you when Papa and I aren't around."

There she was again, talking about God. I told her about T.C. She thought it was pretty funny that I should mistake him for God.

Papa had raced off to check a sow who was due to have babies soon. When he was out of sight, Mama pulled a bottle of milk out of her jacket pocket. She had not forgotten me. I sucked out every drop.

"Don't tell Papa," she smiled. "He'll just say, 'you're spoilin' that pig rotten'." I love Mama.

The warm milk made me sleepy. The next thing I knew it was morning. I had slept all night.

The rays of the morning sun seemed to turn my straw pile into golden threads. Surprisingly, the straw pile was a mighty fine bed.

Sometime in the night a quiet visitor had crept into my pen. There on the straw, curled in a ball, lay a tuckered out Tom Cat, sound asleep.

Chapter 5.

A CURE FOR LONELINESS

PAPA came by early. As soon as he checked my food and water he made a quick exit. T.C. headed out to find breakfast as soon as his eyes were open. So here I am, just me and myself.

The day dragged on and on ----and on. Hours seemed like days! By the middle of the afternoon I was so lonesome --I felt sick! My head hurt! My belly sounded like buzzing bees! But most of all I felt as if I had been deserted. Where were my friends? Other hogs may get by on food and water only. But me, I need -----companionship. The machine shed was a prison! I was the only prisoner. Everybody else was free to come and go as they pleased, except me!

It was long toward evening when Mama and Mitzi finally showed up. I dug in under the straw pile and refused to come out. Sounds crazy, I suppose. But I felt like hiding from everybody. Confused I guess.

Mama reached into the straw and lifted me out. I refused to look at her. I'd show her, I thought! She flopped down in my pen and loved me up tight in her arms.

"Priscilla, my darling, you haven't eaten a bite. What am I going to do with you? You'll get sick if you don't eat. It's just not natural for a pig to shun food," she cried.

Natural? What's natural? I'm not even sure I'm a pig. But one thing I *was* sure of. I felt ashamed because I had made Mama cry and I knew I was too heavy for her to hold. That's what got me kicked out of the house in the first place.

Wiggling free from her arms I hurried over to my feed box. The pellets did taste better with someone there. I wonder why?

Trying to make me feel better, Mitzi jumped around my pen barking her head off.

"Let's go play in your yard, Priscilla," she begged.

"Be quiet, Mitzi," Mama shouted, "let her eat!"

Having announced that Papa must take a look at me, Mama sped off to find him. My *condition* had really upset her. In her frame of mind she forgot to shut my gate.

Quicker than you can say "spit" I leaped through the open gate. The rear door of the station wagon was open. I jumped right in. Maybe, just maybe, they'd take me back home. Hadn't Mama been sad about my condition? Was it too much to hope for? It would be glorious to be home once again. I lay down in the back seat and cried!

It didn't take them long to find me! When Mama returned with Papa and found my gate open and Mitzi bouncing up and down by the car, it wasn't hard to figure out where I was.

"I can't bear to see her this way," Mama said sadly.

Papa reached in the car and petted my head. "Poor little thing! She's so confused, so unhappy. I hate to take her back inside."

He *can't* take me back to that pig pen, I thought. I moaned and cried and didn't care who saw me. I didn't care about being brave any more. Nobody ever told me about loneliness.

"I can't do this to her, Papa. There has got to be another way. We've taken her from her home. It's not good for her to be alone. She's still a baby. We've expected too much too soon," Mama said. "Let's take turns staying with her for a few days. Mitzi can help us."

Mama's notion sounded awfully good to me. Having company would be the next best thing to going home. I stopped bawling. Mitzi liked the new plan. She volunteered to stay the night.

Papa wasn't too sure about it. "How long can we keep it up?" he asked.

All of a sudden Mama's expression changed. She was getting excited about something, "*I have an idea. It just struck me. I don't know why we didn't think of it sooner.*" Mama was smiling the dandiest smile I had ever seen. Her burst of pleasure was contagious. In fact it was kind of crazy. I started feeling happy and I didn't even know what she was talking about. But I felt something good was in store for me.

"Is it a surprise?" I asked Mama.

"Yes, Priscilla," Mama answered, "and it will come to pass very soon."

"What did she say?" Papa looked funny. It's strange he can't understand me, when Mama can.

"Priscilla wanted to know if it was a surprise," Mama told him. He just shook his head.

It wasn't half bad going back inside knowing Mitzi would be staying the night. Going in, Mama reached in her jacket pocket and pulled out a bottle of milk, right in front of Papa.

"You're spoiling that talkin' pig," Papa grinned.

Papa carried me in. Mama fed me the bottle of milk. Mitzi stayed the night and I was much happier.

Next morning Papa brought food for Mitzi. There was sunshine in his face when he noticed my feed box was empty. I was glad. Sure enough, I had eaten every bite.

For the next few days either Mama or Papa was there during the day. Mitzi stayed the nights. The

Tom Cat came and went. He came when Mitzi went and went when Mitzi came. You know what I mean.

One morning my "parents" arrived bringing all kinds of stuff. They brought lumber, saws, hammers and a bucket of nails. By the end of the day. my pad, as T.C. calls it, was double in size. Now that I'm eating I guess they think I'm going to grow a lot.

During the day the noise of the hammering drove Mitzi and me out to my fenced yard. When Mitzi ran off to play in the orchard, T.C. came down from his perch.

"Hear you're getting a room mate," he said, tossing his head toward the new construction.

"Where have you been? Haven't you noticed that I have a room mate already?" I snapped. I was still aggravated at T.C. for leaving me all alone when I really needed a friend.

"That pooch? She's temporary." He grinned, not seeming to mind my anger. It wasn't my nature to hold a grudge, least of all at a character like this Tom Cat. Before I knew it he had charmed me completely and I was not mad at him anymore.

"What do you know that I don't, Tom Cat?" I asked. I was anxious to hear all about it. "Who will my room mate be? A pig? One my age? Will she like me? Or is it a *he*? And,---"

"Hold it, Pig," T.C. laughed. "If I don't know who it's gonna be, *nobody* knows who it's gonna be.

I'd say, it's the best kept secret on the place. We are all in for a surprise! All I know is this. I overheard your 'Mama' saying it was time to move in a mild mannered hog, now that you are adjusting to your pen."

"Wow! I'm adjusting, I'm adjusting! Did she really say that ---that I'm adjusting? I *want* them to be proud of me." I felt like I was smiling all over. I looked to see if my tail was smiling. I couldn't tell.

"She said it, kid. But ya better hold those giggles. You might not be so happy when another pesky porker invades your privacy."

"I feel too good to be uneasy," I told him. "I'll just wait and see."

Early that same evening things began to happen. There was a commotion in the orchard. T.C. jumped up to the rafters. I shot outside to see what was going on.

I couldn't believe what I saw! There was this big, beautiful sow --walking in front of Mama and Papa! Why did she look familiar to me? She must have been a hundred times my size! Was this my room mate? If this is Mama's surprise, it sure is a big one!

Papa opened my little green gate. *That* sow will never make it through *my* little gate, I thought. But she did. She cleared the gate with room to spare. How *graceful* she is!

I'll bet she could win a beauty contest!

All I could do was stare at her. Finally, I ran inside. I did not know what to say, and even if I did I lacked the courage to say it. She looked so ---elegant! I felt --young and empty headed, but most of all, I was scared.

Mama was watching me. I knew she was concerned. I tripped clumsily over to the corner, stood behind my straw pile, and watched. The sow gave me a pleasant glance.

T.C. called down to me from the tractor seat. "You're lucky, Porker." I wondered what he meant by that. Am I lucky or am I not?

I didn't take my eyes off the new resident. She tried to eat some of my pellets but my feed box was too small for her mouth. Papa snickered about that. "Don't worry, Hotsie, I'll bring in your feeder and some sow pellets," he said. Well! It was quite apparent that Papa favored this sow. He called her "Hotsie". A feeling burst forth in me that I had never felt before. I was jealous. And I was reasonably sure that this was the sow that Papa calls his queen, the one he shows off to all his friends.

Everybody was bossing me. "Talk to her, Priscilla," Mama said. Papa said the same thing. Even Mitzi was telling me to be more friendly. The idea! I didn't feel like being anything, ----except a spectator. Why are they rushing me?

T.C. sat on his perch looking disgusted, the thing he does best. But I knew he loved the excitement.

Would Hotsie make fun of me too, like the other sows did? Could it be that she was in the farrowing barn that day when they all laughed at me and called me names? She *probably* was.

Papa brought in a round rubber tub for Hotsie's water and a big "V" shaped wooden box for her pellets. My, she must eat a lot, I thought. Then Papa emptied a sack of sow pellets in her feed box. Her pellets were a lot bigger than mine. No wonder she's so fat!

Mama came in and gave me a hug. "Give her a chance, Priscilla," she said, in a kind, quiet voice. "She won't harm you. It's not her nature. If you like her, I'll leave her here. If you *don't* like her ---we'll give you a few days to make up your mind and then I'll make sure Papa takes her out."

I wanted to make Mama proud of me but I could not help asking. "Won't I ever get to go home with you again Mama?"

"This is your home now darling," she said. "You are getting older and larger each day. You have already made considerable progress here, but you have lots to learn yet about your own kind. You can learn from Hotsie and *you must learn* before you grow up." Mama hugged me one more time. Then she and Papa left. I was plenty worried.

"You need not be afraid of me, Priscilla," Hotsie said. "I'm here to keep you company and assist you in any way I can. Are you Mabel's daughter? Are you the one who's been living in the house?"

Here it comes. She's pumping up her lungs to blast out at me! To heck with her! I just won't answer her questions!

"Don't be afraid of me," she repeated. "You talk to me when you are ready." She walked out in the yard and lay down on my favorite lying down place. *Some nerve!*

Chapter 6.

LEARNING AND SHARING

TOM CAT dropped in, in somewhat of a huff. In fact, he commenced to throw a real fit. "Priscilla! Is your brain out to lunch? What's the matter with you? You're lucky! You get a rose for a room mate. And what do you do? You treat her like a prickly prune! You've got a problem! You, you are the one who was so all fire worried about other porkers liking you. So, what do you do? You're nasty to the first one you meet, who, by the way, happens to be the finest hog on the place!"

"But nobody told me she was coming!" I said. "They just 'sprung' her on me. All of a sudden *here she was! What was I supposed to do?*"

"Be *friendly*. Your Mama has gone to a lot of trouble for you, Porker. Look at this! A whole new

38

wing added to your pad just so *you* can have some company! And Hotsie, she's a good ol' girl! Everybody likes Hotsie!"

What have I done? The Tom Cat would not lie to me about such an important matter. I had it coming. Bawling me out was letting me off too easy. He probably should have slugged me. I was so ashamed of myself. I hurried out to the yard to try to make amends, but Hotsie was asleep.

"She's asleep," I whispered to T.C.

"She won't sleep forever," he answered.

Maybe not. But it sure seemed like it. I kept on watching the big sow, hoping she took short naps. No chance! She slept and snored and snored and slept some more.

Meantime I got to thinking about what she had asked me, if I was Mabel's baby? I think she already knows.

Watching the sow sleep made me sleepy too. I fluffed up my straw and fell asleep, but as soon as Hotsie begin to stir ---I woke up.

She was noticeably slow about getting up. But then, there's a lot more of her to get off the ground. Her "start ups" take longer than my "get ups".

"Good morning," I said, not knowing what else to say. It was my first try at being polite to a hog and I wasn't about to blow it this time.

Hotsie smiled at me. "Good morning," she

answered.

"It really isn't morning you know. You just took a long nap." Couldn't have her think that I didn't know night from day.

"I'm pleased you are talking to me, Priscilla. Perhaps my questions earlier bothered you. You must think me quite nosey. I didn't mean to pry into your affairs." Hotsie said softly.

"Oh! That's all right," I answered quickly. "I have a lot to learn about myself. You guessed right about me. That old sow, Mabel, she *was* my mother, but *not* anymore." From Hotsie's expression I could see I had shocked her. "Did Mama and Papa put you in here to teach me to act like a pig?" I giggled.

Hotsie didn't answer. She just stared at me with her mouth wide open. The poor sow! I guess she was trying to figure me out.

"Mama and Papa?" she questioned. "Is that what you call the Mr. and Mrs.?" I don't think she was judging me. If she was annoyed I could not detect it. Her questions had the sound of surprise and somewhat like she was trying to solve a riddle. I was the riddle!

"I've *always* called them Mama and Papa. They were my 'parents' while I was growing up, and still are. You gonna yell at me about it?" I asked, feeling sure she would! But then I got the surprise of my life.

"Priscilla! Why should I *yell* at you for something

as lovely as that? We are fortunate to have the Mr. ----
or that is, your Mama and Papa to care for us. We are
fortunate indeed."

Hotsie made me feel *stu---pen---dous.* "Oh, thank
you, Hotsie. Thank you." I said.

"For what, Little One?" she asked.

"For not yelling. For understanding why I call
them Mama and Papa. I *do* love them so." I was so
happy I cried.

I had misjudged Hotsie and I must learn to never
do anything like that again. Hotsie could not have
been one of the old sows in the farrowing barn who
called me names and made fun of me. No sir! Not
her! She's far too fine.

There was a muffled sound of applause above me.
I had forgotten about the Tom Cat. He was sitting in
the tractor seat, peering down. By the silly look on
his face I could tell he hadn't missed a single word.

"See? What did the ol' tabby tell ya, huh? Huh?"
he snickered. "Yeah," he strutted about, "you and
Hotsie ought to hit it off *real* good." When T.C. was
pleased with himself he was down right disgusting.
"Well, ta-ta," he said, "I'll be off. Got a couple of
anxious cuties waiting for me. Don't want to be late
---- or press my luck." Thank goodness, he left.

Everyone was right about Hotsie. No time had
passed, or so it seemed, until I understood why Papa
called her his "queen". I could see why Tom Cat

called her the "nicest hog on the place". She truly is a
queen and a splendid one at that.

I didn't know how dumb I was until Hotsie began
sharing endless stories about hogs and how they live.
She talks about growing up with her brothers and sisters, about life in the feeder barn and farrowing barn.

I think *I'm* dumb because I know so little about
hogs. Yet, Hotsie thinks I'm ever so bright. She seems
to feast on my past adventures. She loves to hear
about television shows and birthday cakes adorned
with pretty lighted candles, about the time I got to
run in the soft beach sand and watch the sun magi-
cally disappear into the ocean.

Each time I tell her a story from my past she
says, "To think that a pig could do such a thing! You
must remember it always and tell it to your children
and your children's children." Actually, Hotsie and I
were teaching each other.

Papa once said I wouldn't last ten minutes with a
batch of hogs. At that time his words meant very little to me. But now because of Hotsie's teaching, I
understand. Pigs fight a lot! When they feed off their
mother, they squabble over choice nursing spots.
Can't prove it by me! I don't remember ever getting a
nursing spot, choice or otherwise.

Older pigs find other things to fight about, such
as feed, resting spots and a lot of other silly stuff like
that.

If I had been poked right into a pen of pigs, they would have clobbered me. What do I know about fighting? Papa was right in his judgment. Not that I'm a coward. Papa knows I'm not! But so far, I've never had to bite or kick anyone to get the things I need.

I know almost nothing about my brothers and sisters. *Their* mother raised *them*. Hotsie said they were moved to the feeder barn when they were five weeks old. When they grow up they will be pig producers either here or on some other farm.

Hotsie enjoys telling about other farmers who visit here shopping for breeding stock for their farms. She likes the way Papa shows off each sow. He calls them by name and describes in detail the sows' fine qualities.

One thing for sure, Hotsie favors Papa. "He treats me like I'm part of the family too, Little One," she said happily.

"Were you born in the farrowing barn?" I asked.

"No," she answered sadly, "I wasn't that lucky."

My curiousity was aroused. "Where did you come from? How did you get here?"

"Your Mama saw me at an auction," she said cheerfully.

"At an *auction? You* were taken there to be *sold? How* did you *get* there? Who would ever want to sell you?" I couldn't believe my ears!

"Thank you, Priscilla, for caring about me. But

you see, the Deerfields owned me first. They were different from the Mr. and Mrs.! Mr. Deerfield fed us, but not regularly. Many times he threw our feed right down in the mud. While we all competed for a mouthful, it was trampled into the ground and became feed only for the earthworms."

"How awful!" I said, feeling sorry for her.

"I didn't know if I should be glad or not when I heard that the Deerfields were selling us." She continued. "I'd never lived anywhere else. I had no idea there were farms like this one and people who love hogs like your Mama and Papa."

"Did you have your own pen at the Deerfields?" I asked.

"Not hardly! Twenty seven of us shared a big muddy lot. When the weather was bad, we all tried to squeeze into a leaky little shed. Once in a while, if lady luck smiled on me, I'd get to sleep part of the night inside."

"Golly, Hotsie, I'm sure glad Mama went to that auction. Did she bring you home in the pick-up truck?"

"She sure did! I had the truck *all* to myself and slept *all* the way home," she laughed. "Do you know what your Mama said to me when I got on the truck?"

"Something nice, I'll bet." I answered, knowing how Mama talks to hogs.

"She said, directly to me, 'How could anyone sell you? I never could. Underneath all that mud, I can see a beautiful Chester White sow'. No one had ever talked to *me* before! Then she said, 'Lie down in the truck, darling. We'll be home soon'."

"That sound like Mama. She calls me darling too!" I said. "I'm glad you went to that auction, Hotsie!"

"So am I! And I'm glad your Mama was there!"

No wonder Hotsie likes Papa, after the way she was treated before. "That mean old Mr. Deerfield!" I just couldn't help saying it.

"That's all in the past," she said tenderly.

We pushed our straw beds close together.

"Good-night, Little One," she said.

"Good-night, Hotsie," I answered.

Why couldn't Hotsie have been my mother? She would never have lain on me. Suddenly, as I looked at her, I remembered where I had seen her before! I was sure of it! She was the beautiful white sow in my dream, the one who saved my life. Of course!

"Good-night," I whispered. But she was asleep.

Papa must never separate us.

Chapter 7.

HOTSIE MOVES OUT

HOTSIE is due to have her pigs in ten days. So anxious about the new litter, she talks constantly! Endless tales. About past families. Each little fellow is fondly mentioned. She seems to relish the telling.

I've listened most politely to her reminiscing, no matter how many times she repeats the story. I adore her. Each day she grows greater in size and in beauty and surprisingly, more graceful. Oh, to be like her, some day.

I know our time together has almost ended. For ordinarily a sow is hurried off to the farrowing barn a full two weeks before she delivers. But Papa knows his Hotsie is better satisfied here, with me. After all, with so many sets of pigs to her credit already, Papa says she has a "doctorate degree" in pig production.

Hotsie isn't the *only* one who's putting on weight.

46

Time was when Mitzi's five pounds were more pounds than I had. But now ----just a few months later ---she still weighs five pounds, and *I weigh a hundred and seventy-five!* Not even Papa can lift me now! The other day I accidently stepped on Mitzi. Boy! Did she let out a yelp? But she brought it on herself, darting around between my legs, barking, acting silly, showing off how small she is!

"Priscilla! You'd better go on a diet!" she barked.

In spite of the misery I had inflicted on the poor little dog, I had to laugh. Hotsie laughed too. T.C. laughed loudest. From high above us, he snickered one of his nasty snickers. Still, he's overjoyed by anything causing the dog pain.

I *am* heavy. That's a fact. Growing is what I do best. I'm not sure about this growing up business. Hotsie said when I reach one hundred and ninety pounds they will move me to another barn for my breeding. I'll reach that weight in no time! When it comes to eating, I'm such a pig!

This morning, Mama hurried in with a tiny brown radio tucked under her arm. Without so much as a "good-morning" she marched toward a small shelf near my pen, and set it down.

How wonderful! A radio for me! The farm house was always alive with music. Country and western in the mornings, along with the live stock and crop report. We listened to the Boston Pops on Saturday and the Mormon Tabernacle Choir on Sunday. My favorite was banjo pickin'. Made me feel like jumpin' around.

Mama was acting strange. She slipped out the door without a word. Didn't even turn the radio on! What's worse ---she forgot my bottle of milk! Maybe I'm to big to complain about the milk, but I *feel like* complaining.

Mama keeps on sneaking me that bottle of milk.

They play some kind of a game. Because, Papa knows. One morning he came in with an innocent smile on his face and a bottle of milk in his pocket.

"Mama has gone to town to get a permanent," he said joyfully, as he held the bottle over the fence to me. The milk was just as sweet as always. I drank it down without shame and thanked him properly for his kindness. But unlike Mama, he didn't understand a word I said.

T.C. makes fun of me. He says I should be ashamed of myself to suck a baby's bottle, at my age. *Ask me if I care. I don't! Not a bit!* As long as Papa and Mama take pleasure in fetching it to me, I will take appropriate delight in drinking it.

Hotsie was napping in the yard. I was anxious to tell her about the radio.

Suddenly, it dawned on me why Mama had brought the radio and why she was avoiding me. I'd bet my supper that *today,* is the day, Hotsie gets moved. The thought sickened me. I stood in the doorway for a while and looked at her lying there, my friend and teacher. They can't just up and take her away from here. Can they?

Before long I knew that betting my supper would have been a safe bet. Already, Papa stood by Hotsie, coaxing her to get up. I could not hold back the tears!

"Please, please don't take her," I blubbered.

"I'll never ever see her again!"

"Of course you will, darling," Mama said as she kneeled down and put her arms around my neck. "I'll make sure of it. Hotsie has to go now, Priscilla. You know she does. You wouldn't want her to be unprepared when her children arrive, would you?" Mama said tenderly.

"Let her stay *here* and have her pigs!" I begged. "There's plenty of room," I cried, racing around the outermost edges of the pen. "Just look at all this room!"

Again, Papa called to Hotsie. She inched up and slowly turned toward me. A single tear, trickled down her face.

"I *must* go, Little One. And *you* must be brave. You will be coming down to the big barn, real soon. We'll see each other. Your Mama will see to it." She didn't say "good-bye" and I couldn't either.

The loyal sow followed Papa through the little green gate. A tight squeeze. I watched them cross the orchard. When they were out of sight, I sank to my knees and cried like a baby.

"The end has not come, Priscilla," Mama said, stroking my head. "I know you will miss Hotsie, but you still have the rest of us."

As a matter of course the Tom Cat had been watchman to Hotsie's departure. Mitzi had trailed along behind. Knowing that, the cat dropped in.

"You see! Here is one friend dropping in already," Mama said, trying to make me laugh. Next, she turned on my radio. I was in no mood for music, but I did not want to be troublesome.

Mama stayed for a long time. She brushed me and rubbed me down with oil. T.C. hung around all day. When evening came, Mama returned with Mitzi. Mitzi spent the night.

A week past before I stopped feeling sorry for myself. Then I began to realize how selfish I'd been. I wanted Hotsie to stay and keep me company, forgetting all about the whole new family she must soon care for.

I confided in Mama. Telling her how ashamed I was for being so selfish. Mama understood. She was easy on me. She said everybody is selfish sometime. Knowing that sort of gave me back my self respect.

The Tom Cat became a regular Pony Express for Hotsie and me. First thing every morning he was prompt with a bit of news from her.

One morning I waited and waited for him to come, but he didn't show up! In fact, nobody came! Nobody! By mid-afternoon I had imagined all sorts of things and was about as worried as a body can be.

Darn this pen! If I was free to run loose like that cat I wouldn't have to wait to be visited. I could do some visiting, myself. I had an idea.

I took a hard look at the little green gate. If I

wanted to I could break it down! And, *I wanted to!* That's what I'd do then. I'll rush the gate and go crashing right through!

I started warming up like athletes do, by pacing around my yard. With each turn I picked up speed! I ran faster and faster until I was sure I had reached the right speed for breaking down gates. I gritted my teeth, ducked my head, closed my eyes and yelling "CHARGE" ------------I ran for the gate!

Suddenly, a wild furry ball hit me in the head! Ker-Wham! I was stopped in my tracks! I saw shooting stars and pick up trucks! Then I saw the Tom Cat propped up on his front feet. His eyes looked funny. First they rolled round and round, then up and down. Mercy me! Somewhere between my bright idea and the gate I had charged the Tom Cat!

"Whatza --happen?" the cat sounded drunk.

And I felt ridiculous. I really blew it. Meant to ram the gate! Instead, I rammed the Tom Cat. Disgusting! So was the cat hair ---stuck to my nose.

"First, you think you're people! Now you're acting like a billy goat!" T.C. managed to say. He was up. On shaking legs.

"I ----I'm sorry. I was --well ----I was going to knock down my gate," I admitted. Saying it, sounded really dumb. "I got lonesome and worried," I said, trying to justify my actions.

Still cockeyed, T.C. grinned. "Oh, that's right!

You haven't heard the news! You clobbered me before I got a chance to tell it!"

"News?" I tried to blow the cat hair off my nose. "What news?" It made me sneeze. "I haven't seen a soul!" I said, hoping I had gotten rid of all the furry stuff.

"Your old friend, Hotsie, her little porkers were born. Sixteen wee ones! Took her all night! Wasn't easy, but she came through for your Papa. He's got somethin' new to brag about!"

"Sixteen? Really? Sixteen? Ter--rif--ic!" I jumped up and tried to click my heels, but I couldn't. "No wonder Papa calls her the Queen."

"Well, she's a plum tuckered out queen this morning. Her majesty ain't as young as she used to be," he said.

"Is that where you've all been? With Hotsie?" I asked. "Mama and Papa too?"

"All night and all morning," he answered. "But they will be here in a minute."

"I'm sorry for crashing in to you like that, Tom Cat," I said shyly.

The cat burst out laughing and seemingly recovered, he took off for his perch in the rafters. I'm glad he's laughing about it. Maybe I will be able to laugh about it someday.

Papa dragged in, needing a shave, and carrying a bucket. Mama hadn't looked so tired since I was a baby, when she gave me night feedings. Nevertheless, they both were happy and excited.

"Have you missed us, Priscilla?" Mama asked. *Of course* I missed them, but she didn't wait for an answer. "Sorry we couldn't visit you this morning, but Hotsie needed us. Someday, when you become a mother, we will all be there to help you too. Then you'll understand."

I understand already! Hotsie told me about *those things!*

Mama checked my feed box. I still had plenty. She threw out my stale water and gave me some fresh.

Papa was up to something. He was wearing his "up to something" face. He clutched that bucket like it was worth a lot of money. Then he set it down gently in my pen. I wandered over to take a peek inside. Papa tipped the bucket. Out jumped a squealing pig! It startled me! I bolted backwards! The pig ran straight toward me! I ran the other way, keeping an eye on it! Mitzi thought it was funny. She laughed at me. So did Mama and Papa. I felt foolish. What a dirty trick to play on me!

I whirled around and told the pig to mind its own business. It stopped short, dropped to the floor and hung its little head.

Now, I've really done it! How could I be so thoughtless to hurt its feelings like that? What would

Hotsie think of me? I know this pig belongs to her.

"Don't you like him, Priscilla?" Papa asked, sadly. "I think he likes you."

So, it's a "him" is it? "Him" just sat there and looked at me. He made squawking noises. I tried to explain to everybody that I had never seen a baby pig before and had been taken quite by surprise. I was the victim of a very bad joke.

The pig didn't look a bit like Hotsie but he *was* *cute*. His coat was a glossy black except for a wide white band around his middle.

He popped up again making more noise than ever. I swear, he sounded like a duck! How could a child of Hotsie be such a nuisance?

A horrible thought occurred to me. What if all baby pigs are like that! Poor Hotsie! Sixteen to care for! Wow! No wonder Papa calls her a queen! And to think, *I'm being groomed for motherhood.*

Papa reached in and picked up the pig. "Time to go back to your mama," he said.

"Thank goodness," I said.

At last, Mama gave me a sympathetic glance. I hoped it meant she was sorry for letting Papa spring that pig on me, so unexpected. I'll find out how sorry she is. I'll ask her for a favor, something *special* to eat. Perhaps grapes! I love grapes! I asked; it worked! She promised she would buy some at the store.

Sixteen? What will I do with babies?

Chapter 8.

AN ARGUMENT

THE nanny goats play an important part in Papa's pig production. And, in Mama's pig "saving" operation too.

It was *goat* milk in that first bottle she gave me and *goat* milk in the last.

Only two nannies live here on the farm. Each gives about five to six quarts of milk a day. The milk is *never* used in the house. Mama rations it out --------- like a precious vitamin elixir. Only the needy ever get a taste.

The very fact that I'm sneaked a bottle of this choice stuff everyday, leads me to believe that I rate high as heck, with Mama. That bottle of milk means as much to me as her evening pan of popcorn means to her.

The nannies are called Patches and Gertie.

Patches is a multi-colored, flop eared nubian. Her

lovely coat demands immediate attention. It looks exactly like a patch work quilt --without the stitches. Her name fits just fine.

Patches is always chewing. Most of the time, part of what she's chewing is spilling out one side of her mouth. Nasty looking!

Gertie is a creamy white saanen. Unlike Patches, she has horns. Well --nearly, anyway. She *should* have a nice white matching pair, or none at all. But Gertie is different! She has one long horn pointing to her rear and one stub that just sits there, being short! Whoever tried to make her hornless, sure flubbed the job. Poor thing. Papa and Mama bought her at an auction. Nobody else wanted her because her horns look so strange. She may have strange looking horns, but her milk is delicious!

One morning, a few days after Hotsie's delivery, I was awakened by a thundering argument! It came from the orchard and got louder every minute! The nannies? Arguing? I could hardly believe it! They always appear to be the best of friends. But here they were, yelling and screaming at each other!

Sounded to me like a clear case of jealousy.

Some of Hotsie's pigs are being fed a slug of that goat milk, a couple of times a day. I don't mean to imply that *her* pigs are weaklings, but with so many mouths to feed, she can use all the help she can get.

Patches claims her milk is far superior to Gertie's.

"Face it, Gertie! You are over the hill! Antiquated! Old! Real old! Your milk is clabbered! A baby pig would choke to death on it."

How could Patches be so cruel? This was a side of her I had never seen. In spite of it all, Gertie held her own.

"Wonderful! You've noticed that I'm older. Then mind your manners, young lady! Show some respect! My full development and contented nature give me the edge. Everyone knows milk is better, much better, when it comes from a contented goat. I am blessed with quietness of mind and peacefulness of spirit, the very thing you lack."

"What difference does it make whose milk is the best?" I asked them.

I should not have asked! Gertie stomped her foot in protest. Patches gave me a "mind you own business" stare.

"Don't bother with them," T.C. told me. "They have this very same argument every time Hotsie has pigs."

"Well, it's news to me. I've never been around before when Hotsie had pigs!" I replied. "What's going on here? I thought the nannies were good friends!"

"Don't worry about it, Porker. This will all blow over in a day or two. It always does! You have to understand; Hotsie is their favorite. Patches wants only her milk to go to Hotsie's pigs because she *really* does believe her milk is the best. Gertie --well, you heard the argument. She thinks her milk is best." T.C. Explained.

"In other words, they want only the best milk for Hotsie's babies?" I asked.

"*Right,*" he answered.

"Tom Cat, I think I just fell in love with two nanny goats!" We both held our stomachs and rolled with laughter.

Chapter 9.

ALL GROWN UP

TODAY is my *big* day! I have finally reached the magic weight of 190 pounds. *That* makes me eligible for the big barn. The one for *adult* hogs, like me.

Mama promised I could see Hotsie and her pigs the moment we arrive at the barn. However, that promise was made several weeks ago. For some reason *I failed to gain weight as quickly as I was supposed to*. Hotsie's pigs have been weaned and moved to the feeder building. Papa couldn't keep them with their mother ----just for me. I will *never* see them. As for Hotsie, Mama assured me that I can see her.

T.C. was unusually quiet. Maybe the old fox is sick! Somehow, I can't picture *him* "unhealthy". I know where he is. He's perched in the rafters, where he always is when something is going to happen that he doesn't want to miss.

"Come on down, Tom Cat. Keep me company. This is my big day, you know. It's graduation day! I'm movin' on up with the grown-up," I said proudly.

The cat did not answer. Maybe he *is* sick!

"Don't you feel well?" I called up to him.

"Certainly I feel well. Did you ever know me to feel otherwise?" he spouted. Giving an example of his vigor, he climed to the highest point above my head. He looked down to make sure I was looking up. Then the show began, and so did the show-off. He leaped, he jumped, he sprang and he fairly flew from rafter to rafter, again and again. The darn fool! It made me dizzy trying to keep an eye on him. Why did I ask if he was sick?

"Please come down from there! I'm leaving this place today!" I said. "Frankly, I'm scared. Come on, T.C. They'll be here any minute to take me away."

For his finale he sprang again to the highest point and bowed himself to me. Then, he dived, a graceful, most elegant dive, landing squarely and softly on the tractor seat.

There was nothing plain or simple about this cat! He had made his point. He was not sick!

"It won't be easy for you, Porker," he said, showing no sign of exhaustion.

"Moving? Are you worried about me?" I asked.

"Matter of fact, I am," he retorted.

"You needn't, Tom Cat. I'm all grown up now."

"That's what you think! Since the day you were born your Mama and Papa have pampered you, given you special treatment, and spoiled you. I've watched 'em. They mean well. But now it's going to be different. Those old sows will show you no mercy," T.C. said quietly.

My mind was all mixed up. The cat made me worry. Maybe I'm not all grown up. But I've learned to live in a pig pen, sleep on straw, eat what pigs eat, and I don't drink from a baby's bottle any more, not after I noticed how much bigger I was than Hotsie's baby pig. I couldn't bear the thought that I might be taking milk from one of Hotsie's babies. Boy! Was Mama surprised the day I turned my nose up to a bottle of warm goat milk and said, "I'm too old for that."

Mitzi tore in, barking. Mama and Papa would not be far behind.

"I get to walk through the orchard with you, Priscilla!" Mitzi said excitedly.

"Who asked you to?" the Tom Cat snickered.

Can you beat that? Tom Cat actually spoke to Mitzi! Wouldn't it be wonderful if they became friends. But, that's too much to hope for.

"That cat spoke to me! Even if it was a rotten remark --he still spoke to me," Mitzi said.

"If you stop chasing Tom Cat, he might be more friendly toward you," I said to Mitzi. Knowing T.C. was listening, I decided a little sugar on my words, couldn't hurt. "He is a remarkable cat and will return kindness with kindness. Just try and see! He is *my friend*. A real good one too; loyal and trustworthy," I said.

Suddenly, Mama and Papa were there. I felt shy and awkward. Mama came in and sat down on my straw bed. Papa shut off the radio. I wish he hadn't. No one said a word. I wish they would. My heart thumped like tennis shoes in a clothes dryer.

"It's time to go," Papa said.

"Just give us a few minutes, Papa," Mama told him.

I figured Mama had something important to tell

me.

By this time the idea of being moved in with strangers had me about half scared to death. I wanted to tell Mama, but I did not want to be troublesome.

"You're a big girl now my Priscilla, but you still have a lot to learn. The sows in the farrowing barn may scare you at first. If they seem crude, vulgar, ungraceful or barbaric, just remember, they were raised by 'good' mothers who taught them how to survive.

"Papa and I will never be very far away. In fact, you will see more or us in the big barn. That's where most of our work is. Now here's the good news! As soon as we get there I'll take you right straight back to Hotsie's pen."

Thinking about seeing Hotsie bolstered my courage. Mama and I followed Papa. So did Mitzi. About half way across the orchard I looked back. T.C. was slithering gingerly through a space in the fence. Mitzi saw him too.

Mitzi stopped for a second and stared at the cat.

Tom Cat kept coming.

I watched, hopefully!

Tom Cat called out to Mitzi, "Truce?"

Mitzi looked to me for an answer. I would not give it. She must decide.

With obvious reluctance she said in a low voice, "Truce."

I suggested that she say it louder.

"Truce!" she repeated, this time more sure of her answer. "I won't chase your friend anymore, Priscilla," Mitzi told me.

She means it! The Tom Cat must have known too. By the time we reached the farrowing barn, my two friends were walking side by side.

As for me, I grew more nervous with each step!

Chapter 10.

A NEW HOME FOR ME

ONCE we reached the barn door my desire to rush right in vanished like a pitcher of lemonade on a hot summer's day. Inside was the unknown. At least it was unknown to me and that was scary.

Remembering what happened the last time I stood in this doorway made me uneasy and suspicious. Just thinking about those hateful old sows gave me a headache. Why were they so cruel to me? I was just a little pig! Was it all because I had had the good fortune to live in the house? Their merciless words pierced my heart that day and made me cry.

Now that I'm older, maybe they won't recognize me. Not much chance of *that* I suppose! No doubt, the word is *out* about my moving *in*.

Nevertheless ----I'm still me. Live in the house I did and that fact I am not ashamed of no matter how

67

much they try to humiliate me.

It was plain to see why the farrowing barn was also referred to as the "big" barn. Once inside, the spaciousness seemed to swallow us up. The machine shed was tall, but this one sprawled ----straight ahead!

There was a wide hallway covered with more of those sweet smelling wood shavings. The hallway divided two rows of pens that connected end to end and appeared to go on forever. In front of each pen was a fresh bale of wheat straw for bedding.

We looked like a parade as we filed into the barn. Papa marched ahead calling out directions to us. Mama and I tramped along behind, paying very little attention to Papa.

Sniffing here and there at everything of interest to them, Mitzi and T.C. dawdled well behind. The truce was still in effect. It was too good to last. Any minute now I expected them to switch back to their true characters and commence firing on each other.

The front pen to our left was empty. On the door ------no, I mean on the gate! I must not even think *people* words and *never* speak them, except to Mama of course, and not even then, if a hog is listening!

On the "gate" of the pen hung a small sign with shiny black letters. Mama pointed to the pen.

"See there, darling," she said. "This is your new pen. See? Your name is on it already. You will only be in this pen --part of the time, and part of the time you'll be back in the machine shed."

Part of the time? I wondered what she meant by that, but I didn't ask. I'll save my questions for Hotsie. She'll clue me in on all the details of adult hog living.

Mitzi darted wildly ahead of us. In fact, she got right in our path and started a ruckus. We had a choice. We could either stop or run over her, rough-shod! Naturally, we stopped.

My little friend set to work performing her loud-est protest. She barked so hard she bounced clean off the ground. Figuring out what she wanted was not too difficult for anybody.

"Stop that infernal racket, dog! You'll wake up all the baby pigs!" Papa hollered, making a lot more thunder than the dog.

Good ol' Mitz! She was looking out for me, afraid I'd be funnelled directly into my new pen without seeing Hotsie. I knew she was worried for nothing. Mama had promised. There were no two ways about it. We were heading straight for Hotsie's place.

Papa and Mitzi had set up quite a commotion. Although it was they who made all the racket, it was I who caught the brunt of it. I'd swear, every eye in the place, was on *me!* We were surrounded by hogs, all kinds and colors. One sow to a pen. Some had pigs. Some did not.

We kept walking down the long hallway.

There were white, snub nosed Yorkshires and white Yorkshires with standard noses. The Yorkshires are quite long and deep, and have firm flesh.

It was easy to spot the Chester Whites. Hotsie was the first and the oldest of that breed on the farm. The Chesters have pure white hair and skin. They produce and raise large litters that grow out rapidly. Mama said once that the Chesters are quite mild mannered. I'm sure that's the reason Hotsie was selected to be my teacher and room mate. Mama knew I was *safe* with Hotsie.

The Hampshires are black hogs with white belts encircling their bodies and front legs. Although the Hamps aren't as large as some of the other breeds here, Papa says they are bred for refinement and quality. These sows are very prolific and good mothers.

I can see only a few Durocs. They're the red ones. No two of them are the same shade. The Durocs are large, good mothers and produce great quantities of milk. Papa says they are good crossbreeders and that it wouldn't hurt to have a little Ducoc blood in every pig.

So, far, I haven't spotted one Landrace. That's good. Mabel is a Landrace. I hope I never see *her* again!

Landrace are white like some of the other breeds,

but they are definitely different. Because of their extremely long bodies, they are blessed with an extra set of nipples. Normally, a sow has table settings for twelve or fourteen. A Landrace can serve sixteen pigs at a time.

There's more that's different. The large, droopy ears on a Landrace will make you stop and take a bow. They practically cover the face. And they flop a lot! Come summer, they've got built in sunshades!

Some of what I know about the different breeds I learned from Mama and Papa. But Hotsie told me many things about hogs that humans would never suspect.

As for me, I'm a mixed breed. Papa says I'm one of his specialties, a little bit of this and a little bit of that.

My red color comes from my Duroc grandfather, Nebraska, my white belt from my father, Charles the first, deceased.

I inherited some, not all of the Landrace length. Thank God! I did not inherit the elephant ears!

As we passed by the pens, I hoped someone would say, "Hello", or "Nice to see you", or "Welcome". Maybe hogs don't do those things. Mostly, they stared at me as if to say, "There *she* is". Some of them paid no heed to us at all. I liked that. A couple of them had their heads together and goggled after me with disfavor.

I glanced about for means of escape just in case the sows were planning something ----like in my dream! There were only two doors. The one at the far end of the hall looked no larger than a peek hole when we came in. From here it looks to be the same size as the front door.

Just then I overheard loud whispers. "She *is* moving in!" someone said. I tried not to care what they said, but I do care.

Please! Please! I thought. Just one kind word of welcome from *somebody*.

I wondered if Mama knew how I felt. Probably not. How could she? I'm the only pig she understands or *thinks* she understands! I'll bet she has the notion that everybody likes me as much as she does, including these old sows. Boy! She sure missed wide of the mark on that calculation! Wonder what she would do if she knew that some of these old gals *hate her Priscilla!* I don't have the heart to tell her.

To heck with this growing up business. If it weren't for seeing Hotsie I'd be more than happy to go right back to the machine shed.

The Tom Cat pulled along side of me.

"How ya doin', Porker?" he asked.

"I don't like this place!" I answered and bounced along.

"Well, ya gotta earn your keep ya know. That means, Porker, ya gotta have a family ----raise some piglets," he informed me.

"Just what do you do to earn your keep, Tom Cat?" I inquired.

"Me? Me? You know what I do! *I keep down the rodent population,*" he bragged. "If it weren't for me this place would be overrun by rats! Those beady eyed creatures would devour your food, contaminate your drinking water, and in the middle of the night when you are sound asleep," he leaned close to me, "they would bite you on the neck." At that moment, as if he had planned it, a fat grey mouse ran across the hall some distance ahead of us. That crazy cat! He flexed his muscles, gave me a nudge and said ---

"Porker, observe!" Quick as a slap he dived upon the frightened prey, sank his teeth deep in its throat and darted off with his catch, out of sight.

"Yuck!" I'm glad that's the way he earns his keep and not me. At least he had taken my mind off the sows. And then, there it was, a friendly face!

"Hotsie!" I shouted. The pen next to hers was empty and the gate was open. I whipped right in.

"Hello, Little One!" she said anxiously.

"Hello, indeed! I'm so happy to see you! But your babies! I've missed them completely! I botched things up. No one's to blame but myself. After you moved out, I couldn't eat! My appetite saddled up and rode away. Mama said she was going to call Dr. Pearon and have him take a look at me. That did it! I didn't want a shot! After she threatened me with the doctor, I ate everything in sight, except the Tom Cat." I laughed.

"Don't worry yourself about it, Priscilla," she smiled, "I'll have more babies before you can stomp a gnat!"

Hotsie hadn't changed a bit, always looking ahead to the next litter of pigs. If that's what it takes to make her happy, then I hope she has tons of them.

But something was wrong. Hotsie's healthy glow had disappeared. She was pale now and definitely not her old self. Nevertheless, she *was* happy to see me. Perhaps our visit will make us both feel better.

Papa and Mama waved good-bye saying they would return, after supper. As they walked away I overheard them talking about Rachel, a sow due to have pigs just any time.

"Have you missed me, Hotsie?" I asked.

"Ever so much, Little One," she answered.

I hoped she had. But with all those babies to care for ----how could she? I took comfort in believing she missed me, a little.

"My name is on the front pen, Hotsie. With me at the front of the barn and you way back here, I'll have to rent a taxi to visit," I complained.

"Don't be sad, Little One," she said. "Before you know it you and I will be together again down at the machine shed."

"Wonderful!" I replied. Knowing my life never seems to proceed as planned I refused to become excited about her remark.

Suddenly, I became aware of a dead silence! Again, I had forgotten about the other sows. Slowly and suspiciously, I peeked around at them. Sure enough! The sows had become sightseers and I was the sight! I'll bet they haven't missed a word we've said. Eavesdropping is *not* nice!

"Hotsie, why are they gaping at me?" I whispered. "Do I look weird? I *am* a crossbreed. Do I have too many crosses?"

Hotsie was furious! Seeing her mad frightened me! With one forceful lunge she rared up, bringing her feet to rest on the top board of the pen! I wasn't the only one frightened. The sows fell into a tizzy, scampering around their pens making nervous grunts and snorts.

Up there, Hotsie was all of eight feet tall, a size demanding attention!

Like a mother would scold a child she shamed the
sows with a cold calculated stare, a most fitting pun-
ishment. When she had gained her composure she laid
her case before them.

"It is *not polite to stare or to listen to private
conversations!* As you can plainly see, Priscilla is no
different than the rest of us. She does not wear a lace
bonnet and silver slippers as some of you suspected!"

She paused for a second and then, in her gentle quiet voice, she said. "Be kind to her! This is her first time in the farrowing barn. I'm counting on each of you to be as friendly to Priscilla as you are to me. Please! Help her adjust to her new surroundings."

She turned and smiled down at me. Then she brought her front feet to rest on the wooden floor. Thud!

She had done it for me! Though the ordeal had taken its toll on her strength, she did not complain. Such a friend!

"A noble gesture, Madam," came a deep voice from across the hall.

"Thank you, Charlie," Hotsie answered.

"Who is *he*?" I whispered.

"He is the gentleman, as *you* would say, who lives across the hall," Hotsie smiled.

"No, I wouldn't say, either," I said quickly. "I will never be able to use people words around the sows. I don't want to get laughed at!"

"Don't be foolish, Little One! You don't have to change your ways just to please others. We only have a few hateful ones here. Most of them are very nice, when you get to know them, especially Charlie."

"It's no use, my friend," I said. "Thank you for believing in me and standing up for me like you did just then. But you might as well save your breath! The sows don't like me. ------They think I'm strange, wouldn't you say? Tell me the truth! Do I look different or is it the way I talk? Or what?"

"Priscilla, there is nothing wrong with the way you look. In fact, you are truly distinguished looking in your lovely red coat with the wide white belt. And surely your Mama has mentioned your adoring, trusting, brown eyes. You Priscilla, are an elegant young gilt. You'll grow up to have lots of pretty pigs!"

Her remark brought a smile to my face. If anyone needed something to smile about right now, it was me. She called me a young gilt. That means a "young lady" in people talk. And, leave it to Hotsie to say I would have lots of pretty pigs! That's what she lives for, larger litters of pretty pigs!

Speaking of pigs, I'll bet hotsie is dying to tell me about her latest family. As soon as I inquired, I could see I had flipped on that magic switch. *In great detail,* she relived that recent part of her life. Long before she was through with the telling, I was through with the listening.

Hotsie looked worn out. Pretending to be sleepy, I suggested we both take naps. Quickly, she agreed.

This pen was not as large as the one in the machine shed, but suitable. It was furnished with familiar items, such as wood shavings, straw, a feed box and drinking water.

A gentle rain made musical tapping sounds on the roof. I thought about my soft pillow behind Papa's and Mama's bed. I could hear the mother sows talking to their babies. I heard eating noises. And whispers! I hoped the whispers were not about me. Feeling very much alone and uneasy, I hid my head from prying eyes, and wept. What would become of me? I want to be accepted by all the hogs. For some reason, that's important to me.

I heard a sow say my name and then laugh. Was she making fun? I wondered. Why don't they just keep quiet!

T.C. slithered in between the 2x4's.

"What ya doin'?" he asked.

"Sh-h," I whispered. "You'll wake up Hotsie! She's awfully pale and needs some rest."

"Is she going to die?" he asked bluntly.

"Die? Don't ever say that!" The thought of her dying had never occurred to me. "She's just tired and pale T.C. ----Papa will see to it that she gets better soon, you'll see."

Mama and Papa were back, doing chores. They made sure everyone had feed, water and bedding for the night. When the chores were finished Mama came in to my pen.

"Priscilla, as soon as you finish eating we are going for a walk back up to your new pen."

"Oh! No! Not yet! *Please* Mama, let me stay here by Hotsie," I begged.

"I don't mean to be unkind to you. I knew you'd want to stay here, Priscilla, but darling, ---you can't. Your old friend hasn't been feeling well. Tomorrow Hotsie will be moved back down to the machine shed where there's more room and peace and quiet. I'm sure you agree we must do everything possible to see she has the best of care."

So --I was right about Hotsie. Mama and Papa are aware of her poor condition.

Nothing seems to go right. Being here in the farrowing barn without her, will not be pleasant.

Not wanting to be troublesome, I hurried with my food. While we ate, Hotsie and I talked through the 2x4's. She promised she would get a lot of rest and get well soon. I promised her that I would be of good cheer and try to make some new friends

Shortly after supper I was whisked away to my new home in the front of the barn.

Chapter 11.

FRIENDS AND ENEMIES

THE hogs were busy with supper when we passed the long line of pens. Even though we poked along while Mama told me the name of a sow here and there, no one paid any attention to me. When a hog eats ----it disregards all else.

Since the sows weren't noticing me, it gave me an opportunity to made some close observations of them.

So many baby pigs! The tiny ones were piled up under heat lamps, sleeping peacefully. They aren't at all like that little pig of Hotsie's, the one Papa dumped into my pen. He ran around quacking like a duck! Poor thing. I guess he missed his mother.

My new pen was like all the others in the barn. I felt sleepy, so I rearranged the straw and sank into it.

Late in the night, the headlights of the car woke

me up. Here in the front pen I can see out the door.

Mama and Papa arrived sleepy eyed, to check on Rachel. Tomorrow is the sow's farrowing date. But she could be early, or late. Rachel had been restless at supper time and was off her feed. In other words, she didn't eat a bite.

I think all the hogs woke up when the car pulled in but they soon went back to sleep. Mama got in the pen with me while Papa checked the sow.

"Didn't mean to wake you, darling," Mama said as she rubbed my head. "You'll get used to us coming and going."

I watched to see what Papa was doing. Not that I didn't like the rub. It felt good. But a rub down I had already had. Being around when baby pigs were about to be born, I had not!

"She's not quite ready yet," Papa said as he climbed into my pen. "She'll keep 'til morning." Papa smiled at Mama. "It's nice to have Priscilla down here ----isn't it? It will take her a while to get used to all the excitement."

Later on, in the night, I heard Rachel scratching at her straw. Making it more comfortable, I guess. I listened for a while and when I couldn't hear her anymore, I went back to sleep.

The next voice I heard was a friendly one, T.C.'s. He was pacing back and forth, by my nose.

"Wake up, sleepy head! You're missing all the

action," he said. Each time he passed by he got a little closer. Finally his whiskers brushed across my snout.

"Wha-What? Where am I?" I jumped up and tried to get my bearings.

"Hotsie has taken up residence in the machine shed. In your absence, I *escorted her* back across the orchard!" he teased.

"Already? How could they do that to me? I didn't get to tell her good-bye!" How disgusting!

"Don't blame your Mama. She and Hotsie came right by here and on out the door. *You were asleep!* That's not all you missed! The Mr. has been here for a long time, with Rachel. She has two little porkers already!" T.C. announced as he stretched out between the 2x4's of the pen.

"Holy heck! Is there anything else?" I felt bewildered.

"Maybe, have you seen Charlie yet?" he asked.

"Yes. He's down at the other end of the barn, in a pen across from the one that Hotsie was in," I answered.

"That's what you think! Your Papa is bringing him up the aisle right now! He's gonna be your neighbor. The sow that was in that pen," he nodded toward the pen on my left, "got moved to another barn already. That was another thing that happened this morning."

Sure enough Charlie moved in next door. He didn't seem to mind the change. He paced the perimeter a few times checking for food and water. The feed box and the water pan were both empty, but he didn't seem to mind that either!

With Tom Cat there and Charlie next door I felt more secure. I turned my attention to Victoria, the Yorkshire sow directly across the hall.

"Is there any word on Rachel's condition?" I asked her.

"Don't be nosey, Greeny!" she spouted. "You wouldn't know, not even if I wasted my time telling you."

Charlie made a strange angry sound. I had never heard anything like it. He shot a glance at Victoria, an *unmistakable* glance. It was most evident, Charlie was not in favor of Victoria's remark.

"I will too, understand," I said, trying to hold my own.

"Keep quiet up there!" yelled the meanest voice I had ever heard. It was a sound of hate and anger. Unless I'm mistaken it was not an older sow, but a young one.

"Don't be cruel, Elsie," Charlie answered. His voice was firm with her and at the same time, quite pleasant. I liked him.

"Well, well, look who's taking up for Little Miss Super Pet," the one he called Elsie said. She flipped her head in our direction. Now, I see her! On my side of the barn, the fourth pen down.

"Tell her off, Priscilla! Do it! Tell her off!" the Tom Cat begged. "Don't let her get away with talking to you like that! Call her names! She did it to you! Elsie is the pits! Call her something nasty."

"How can I, Tom Cat? I don't know anything ---- nasty, to call her. But I have a feeling I'm going to learn pretty darn fast."

"You will, Priscilla, you will!" Charlie said.

"You have been most considerate of me Charlie," I said. "And I thank you for it. .

Of course, Elsie was still listening.

"My! My! would you listen to that! Little Miss Super Pet is giving Charlie the snow job. Maybe she's not so dumb after all." Elsie giggled and then winked at another sow to get approval. The sow was enjoying Elsie's bad behavior.

Once again, Charlie came to my rescue. "Please Elsie, save it! We are disturbing our Rachel."

Somehow, Charlie had managed to perform a miracle. A lull came to rest, over the barn. A soothing calm. And I needed it. The only sounds left were the soft voices of Mama and Papa as they worked with "our Rachel", as Charlie had said.

"What *is* happening back there to Rachel?" I whispered to Tom Cat who had just returned from her pen.

"There's big trouble! The Mrs. has gone to the house to telephone Dr. Pearson. I'll keep you posted, Porker."

Chapter 12.

A STORY FOR RACHEL

IT was a bogus day. Morning dragged into afternoon then on and on into evening. I wanted some company or conversation but decided to keep my mouth shut and stay out of trouble.

Throughout the day Mama and Papa bustled about fussing needfully with Rachel.

I was glad to have the front pen. I can see outside the barn as well as in. There was another advantage. Surrounded by sows? I was not! The front wall of the barn was my left wall, there was a wood wall and windows, to my back, and Charlie was in the pen on my left. The fourth side was a solid gate that opened into the hall and a fence made of 2x4's. My pen is definitely a ringside seat.

At last! Mama came through my gate, walked wearily to my pile of straw, and sort of caved in. She looked positively pooped. I snuggled down beside her to get the full scoop about Rachel. Being ever so quiet, so no one else could hear, Mama told me, just me, about the ailing sow.

"Out of eleven pigs, only two are alive," Mama said sadly. "Dr. Pearson has gone home, Priscilla. He's done all he can do." She began to cry. "Poor Rachel! The doctor said she will be dead by morning!"

"Don't cry, Mama!" I said. "The doctor was wrong!" I couldn't bear to see her cry. "Rachel *has* to live. What would become of her children? Would you take care of them in the house, Mama? You would, wouldn't you?

"I loved living in the house. It was super. But the moving out and growing up, that's what's hard. I still don't know who I am, Mama, pig or people!" I blubbered and cried with her. Then in a moment of weakness, I cut loose and told her all my troubles.

"These old sows don't like me very much," I cried. "I don't know why. I want them to like me. They stare at me and call me names. They think I'm different, and stupid! *Please* let me go home with you! You *know* I would never jump in your lap again. I'll ---------------Oh scrud!"

What is the matter with me!

"Gosh! I'm sorry, Mama! Poor Rachel has a big problem and you feel bad, and all I can think about is myself." I was ashamed.

"My dear Priscilla! I *know* it must be difficult for you. But *you are who you are,* a very special little girl. I don't care how big you get, you will always be a little girl to me. Things will begin to go better. I know they will. You are kind and friendly. Although, it may take them a while, the sows will find you out. Remember Priscilla, these old girls are 100% hog, not 50-50 like you are." She managed to smile. "Now-----about our Rachel. Papa and I are going to spend the night in her pen. We have asked for God's help and I am sure he will give it."

"Will she get better, Mama?" I asked.

"Yes darling, I believe she will. Those two sweet little babies of hers are doing a mighty fine job of re-minding their mother she has something to live for. They're so cute, Priscilla. Papa and I call them Carl and Carlotta." Mama got up. I could see the little rest had helped her. "I'd better go stay with Rachel a while and let Papa have a break."

As soon as I was alone, T.C. jumped down from the rafters scaring the kink clean out of my tail. Made it point to China!

"Don't do that." I shouted.

"Did I scare ya, huh? Did I, huh, did I?" he teased.

"Don't be silly, Tom Cat. Be *serious*, for a change. I have a *serious* job for you. You know about Rachel's condition. (He never misses a thing.) Papa and Mama are trying to keep her alive tonight. We can't just do nothing about it! We've gotta do something to help and I have and idea!

"When I lived in the house I saw a pretty "get well" card that Mama bought for a sick friend. The card had cheerful words on it."

The cat looked perplexed. "Don't tell me you're going to send Rachel a get well card?"

"Not hardly!" I answered. "Where would I get a get well card?"

"Then what have you got in mind, Porker?" he laughed.

"Just this. Rachel must be *completely uncomfortable* by now. There was a time when I was most uncomfortable, but in a very funny way. If I just had someone I could tell the story to, than that person could go and tell Rachel. Of course, it would have to be someone quite bright." I was waiting for the Tom Cat to volunteer! "Do you think you could find me someone bright?" That did it!

"Tell it to *me*. I'm bright! Why, I'm so bright that your Papa carried me around the barn for twenty minutes one night, thought he had the lantern!"

"You crazy cat. I knew I could count on you." What would I do without him, I thought. "Now listen carefully to my story! Don't miss any!"

"I won't," he assured me.

"Make sure Carl and Carlotta can hear the story.

They will surely need cheering too." I added.

T.C. stretched out on the floor and propped his head up with a front paw.

"O.K., Mr. Bright is ready," he grinned. "Lay it on me."

"When I was just a baby, only a week old, Papa and Mama took me in the car with them on a trip to California.

While we were visiting at Irene's house, she's Mama's sister, Diana came. Diana is Irene's daughter-in-law and a school teacher. She teaches little children.

Diana asked Papa and Mama if they would bring me to school so her students could see a pig. Mama didn't think much of the idea, but Diana said all her students are city kids. They had never seen a pig in person. She begged! She insisted, and then she begged some more. Finally, Mama and Papa gave in. They promised we would visit her school the next day.

The promise was kept. Mama carried me into the classroom and Papa brought my bottle of milk. Papa said he didn't want to go walking into school with a baby's bottle in his hand, but Mama talked him into it.

There were lots of kids! Black kids! I had never seen any of that kind before. They all headed straight for me! Mama held me high above her head so they couldn't reach me. They might have pulled my legs off, poked my eyes out and -----well, Diana made them all sit down. I was sure glad about that!

Diana took me from Mama. She was real pretty. She told her students they could take turns petting me, but only one could do it at a time.

Like someone had poked them with a hot stick the kids all stuck up one arm, as high as they could reach. They began waving their hands around, stirring up the air. And take it from me, as stale as the air was in that class room -----it did not need to be fanned.

Diana commenced calling them up to the front of the room to pet me. Some of them giggled, a few called me *cute* and one boy said I looked good enough to eat. I didn't like him.

When the petting ordeal was over, Mama took me back and showed them how I drink from my bottle. Papa was glad to get rid of it. I was thirsty and drank a lot. The kids kept gawking at me. I didn't care about that. Mama put a napkin in the palm of her hand for me to root at. That's the way we did it at home. Those little city kids will grow up believing that all pigs clean their faces on paper napkins."

T.C. laughed at that.

"After about two hours we were lucky enough to make off without a scratch. No sooner had we gotten out the door when another teacher came running up to us.

Diana told us you were bringing Priscilla, she

said happily. 'Would you please bring her in to my class for a few minutes? My students have never seen a real live pig, except on television.'

'Well, I guess it won't hurt. Just a minute though,' Papa said shyly. He didn't really want to do it. Neither did Mama, nor I. But we did it!

What went on in that classroom was not much different than the other one. Except, the teacher told her students I was a piglet. I thought that was funny. I had never been called a piglet before.

Mama stuck the bottle in my mouth again to show the kids how I drank. I didn't want it, but not wanting to be troublesome I drank some down and got my mouth cleaned in the usual way.

The kids were still hollering after us when we left the room. 'Bring her back', they shouted. But we kept on going -----fast!

We didn't run fast enough. Another teacher grabbed Mama by the arm. She put up a fuss. Her children had not seen the pig. So what, I thought. Papa and Mama said no, the little pig has had enough. I couldn't have said it any better myself. Besides, *I had to go to the bathroom, bad*. My kidneys were talkin' to me.

As soon as we stepped into the room the kids started yelling, 'I want to hold the pig,' 'Let me feel the pig,' and every dumb thing they said, made me more uncomfortable.

Papa started yelling. 'Nobody gets to hold the pig and that's final. We'll let ya see her drink milk from her bottle one time and then we're gonna git outa here'.

Oh! No! I thought. Not more to drink. My stomach was about to blow up! Any second! Papa stuck the bottle in my mouth. He wanted to get it over with. So did I. As I sucked a few more drops, my belly swelled up tighter. One of them cleaned my face and before you could say zip, we were out of there.

Mama must have seen my predicament, because as soon as we got to the green grass in the school yard, she put me down. Boy! Was I happy? Relief ----------at last."

The Tom Cat rolled on the floor with laughter.

"Did that *really* happen to you, Porker?" he asked.

"Sure did."

"Did you *really* go with the Mr. and Mrs. on a trip?"

"Yep! I sure did!"

"And you *really* went to school?"

"Yes, and got *very uncomfortable!*" We both laughed some more.

"Mr. Bright" quickly took his leave in the direction of Rachel's pen.

The barn was quiet and dark except for the light of the heat lamps here and there. A pale yellow glow rose from the light in Rachel's pen, where Papa and Mama kept a loving watch on the sow.

Charlie was asleep and so was Victoria. T.C. and I were the only ones, besides Mama and Papa of course, who were up and about.

I suspect Mama and Papa are taking turns sleeping in the lawn chair. They could come down and sleep with me, in my straw. I've slept in their bed! Either one of them would be welcome, I thought, as I fluffed up my bed and lay down.

My mind kept wandering back to my social status among the hog population in the barn. I want so much for all of them to like me. Hotsie told me I shouldn't worry about such things, the other hogs don't. But, I'm not *other* hogs! I'm me! Raised on kindness and cleanliness I was. If fighting and wallowing is the game the sows play then I may never get up to bat!

I've learned something though. Hogs are like people. Some are good, like Hotsie and Charlie. Some are hard to get along with, like Elsie. I wonder how Elsie got that way?

I began to feel sleepy. I hope Rachel likes my "get well" message. When she finds out it's from me, she might not even listen to it!

Chapter 13.

A FIGHT AND A REPORT

JUST before daylight I roused from my bed to get a drink. I saw Papa stowing the lawn chairs and pillows in a wall cupboard. Mama waited for him by my gate. She reached over and gave my head a scratch.

"Rachel is a little better, Priscilla," she whispered. "Isn't that wonderful? She hasn't tried to get up yet but she is eating the food we put by her mouth and drinking the water that Papa funnelled down her throat."

"That *is* good news! How are her children?" I asked.

"Carl and Carlotta are just fine. Although Rachel is quite weak, she has lots of milk, enough for thirteen pigs. With only two pigs to drink it they will be round and robust!"

97

"Carl and Carlotta are lucky to have all that milk for themselves!" I said.

"Papa thinks Rachel is well enough for us to go and get a few hours of sleep. So, bye for now."

"See you," I said and went back to sleep.

When morning came all was calm until a heated argument broke out between Victoria and Lulu. Lulu was Victoria's neighbor. She's across from Charlie.

Before I could figure out what the fuss was all about they had jumped up on their hind legs and, can you believe it, were biting each other over the fence that divided them. How crude! They yelled naughty words to each other.

Victoria got so mad she lost complete control of herself and tried to jump over into Lulu's pen. She almost made it!

Papa heard the commotion and came running in. So did Mitzi. Papa growled at the sows to quiet down.

Mitzi began to whoop it up real loud. Papa hollered
for Mitzi to keep quiet. Victoria and Lulu were carrying on a major battle over the fence.

Poor Rachel! How could they behave so badly
when she is fighting for her life.

Victoria screamed, "I'll get you, you wrinkled
blimp!" Then slap-dash, she jumped the fence! The
two of them ran around the pen eyeing each other.
They took position for organized man slaughter. Or,
pardon me, ----------pig slaughter, that is. The fight was
savage! They bit and they kicked and they stomped
each other. The worst of it all was the squeal, so
sharp that it pierced the morning air. My poor ears. I
may never hear again!

Papa grabbed a shovel, boiled through Lulu's gate and chased Victoria out into the hallway!

"Settle down you, just settle down! Do ya think you're a prize fighter? You look it with that blood all over yourself!" Papa put the big angry sow back in her own pen. Although he shook that shovel at Victoria, I knew he would never hit her with it. The sow probably knew it too. While he checked her over he kept on scolding her for fighting.

I noticed Victoria's foot was bleeding! A real gusher! She seemed to be in a lot of pain, as she limped to her pen.

"What have you done to yourself, hog? That nasty temper of yours has got you into trouble this time," Papa said as he examined her foot. "Besides this bad cut, you've broken your toe! When are you gonna learn to behave yourself?"

Papa didn't see Victoria jump the fence, but I did. Her foot smacked the top board, ker-wham, as she went over.

Both sows were puffin' like it was their first day on the tennis court. Both, were wounded. Lulu was suffering from a bloody torn ear. Victoria bit it! I saw her do it. Yuck! How could she?

Papa checked the ear, put salve on it then gave her thunder for being so contentious.

Lulu is a big red sow with those huge Landrace ears. That makes her a mixed breed, like me. I'm red, but Lulu is redder.

Suddenly, there were shouts of excitement from the rafters from "you know who".

"Come on Rachel! You can do it!" He coached. From up there, T.C. could see better than anyone else. Rachel was trying to get up!

Papa also heard the sow and went flying back to her. "That's a girl, Rachel! Keep trying!"

Then I heard the sweet voices of her little children. "You can do it, Mama. You can do it!" they cried.

The poor sow did try. She rocked back and forth. She kicked her legs again and again, trying to get up, but she just couldn't make it. She lacked the strength.

Papa would be happy she tried. Papa told Rachel she had missed the big fight. I guess she didn't see it, but I'd bet my supper she heard it and that's for sure.

"He's giving her another shot in the hip!" T.C. reported.

Boy, I hate those shots! When I was a baby I got stuck plenty. Papa always gives twice as much medicine as directed. He says if a dose does you some good then a double dose ought to make you get up and dance a jig.

"You just keep trying, sweetheart," I heard him say to Rachel.

When all the excitement was over, T.C. dropped in to bring me word from Hotsie, and I in turn gave him a message for her. The Tom Cat kept me posted on all the *good* news from around the farm but for some reason he was reluctant to report any *bad* news. He had not said a word about Rachel's reaction to my "get well" message. This led me to believe she did not appreciate my humor or my good intentions. I finally asked him about it.

"Oh yeah! With all the excitement going on this morning, I forgot to report!" he said.

"First of all I want you to know your *bright* friend did a superb job of telling the story. A magnificent performance!" he strutted around with his nose in the air. If he had been standing outside in the rain, he would surely drown.

"Do ya wanna know how she took the story? Do ya wanna know, do ya? Huh?" It wasn't like him to tease about something as important to me as this!

"I -----I think I want to know." I answered.

Flashing his broadest grin he proudly announced,

"Priscilla, they loved it!"

For a moment I stared at the cat, uncertain. Was he telling the truth? He could be trying to spare my feelings. He knows how much it means to me to be accepted by the sows.

"Let me tell ya about it, Porker. Last night when I pulled into Rachel's pad the two little ones were catching some z's. They looked real snug in under the heat lamp so I slid in beside them. Rachel was wide awake. I crept over by her and asked if she was in the mood for a get well card. She didn't know what to say! In the first place she is flat on the bricks. Right? And in the second place, she had no idea what a get well card was! I explained it was something you learned about when you lived in the house. At first she acted kinda funny."

"I knew it! I just knew she wouldn't have anything to do with it when you told her it was from me!" I cried.

"Don't jump to conclusions, Priscilla! You ain't heard it all yet. Let me finish, please!" he demanded.

T.C. continued. "I promised Rachel if she would let me give her the get well message, it would make her feel much better. She agreed."

"The poor thing. I don't even know her but I do feel sorry for her. Where were Mama and Papa?" I asked.

"Sitting in one corner of the pen in lawn chairs.

Your Mama was asleep. Now ----let me finish.

I told her the story about you going to school, about the kids, the milk and about your discomfort. At first the sow had an expression of stunned jubilation, as if to say, how could anything like that happen to a hog? Then she began to laugh a quiet laugh as much as her tired body would allow."

"You did it, Porker!" he reported. "You cheered her up. That was a *great idea* you had. --In fact, she liked the story so much she wanted to be sure the pigs got to hear it too. So, I stuck around until they woke up and then repeated the story. Rachel listened to it again. She had another good laugh with her children."

"I'm so glad they liked it," I said.

"Rachel thought the idea of a get well card was an unusually kind expression, for a hog. She said to thank you for your thoughtfulness."

I could feel myself smiling, all over! I'll bet the curl in my tail was smiling too. I looked to see if it was. I think it was.

The Tom Cat knew he had made me happy. "Did she *really* say those things?" I asked slowly. "Did she really?"

"Yes she did, Porker, she *really* did," he said joyfully. Then before I had a chance to thank him, he slithered through my fence and just like the Lone Ranger, out of sight.

Chapter 14.

GOOD NEWS AND A CAST

DURING the night a warm wind blew some beautiful, colored leaves through the front door. Fall has arrived. Each season change is new to me.

I was born in February on the tail-end of winter. By early spring I was moved to the machine shed. Now it's fall, I'm an adult already and not even a year old. Time goes much faster for a pig than it does for a human.

I was afraid the leaves would get raked away with the morning cleaning. But my pen and all the others have been cleaned and the leaves are still in the hall.

"Priscilla, I have a little extra time this morning." Mama said, looking a lot more rested than before. She reached for my brush and a bottle of oil.

"Now don't go to sleep standing up, like you did the last time," she laughed.

106

Mama was right about that. The brushing made me sleepy and I began to lean to one side. All of a sudden I woke up. When I did, I gave myself a quick jerk and shoved Mama ker-smack into the wall.

Mitzi always gets jealous when Mama brushes me. She crawls off to a corner and pouts.

"Why don't you brush Mitzi and put some oil on her?" I asked.

"Never mind Mitzi! She gets bathed and brushed all the time, but *no* oil! If I'd put oil on that dog she would look like a drowned rat!" Mama said. Mitzi did *not* like what Mama said about her.

A rumble of excitement caught our attention. Papa was in with Rachel. The sound came from there. We listened! Mama stood up on my fence to get a better look.

"What's going on down there?" she shouted.

Papa shouted back. "Rachel is just about to make it up! She's trying hard and looking determined."

Mama and Mitzi tore off for Rachel's pen. By the time they got there, the sow was up. She was on her feet, at last.

It was a grand occasion! A time for celebration. The good news traveled like hot lava down a mountain side. It was happy talk. A different type of chatter. Every hog in the place seemed delighted with Rachel's recovery, even Elsie!

The vet won't mind being wrong. Under normal

conditions the sow would surely have died. But here on this farm conditions are never normal! Who else but Papa and Mama would spend the night in a hog pen to save an animal's life? They never give up! And besides, Mama told me that God would not let her die! I wonder how she knew? Maybe that's what faith is. I looked up, and thanked God for helping Rachel.

T.C. was nowhere to be seen. For once he had missed all the excitement. What a shame!

If we held a dance in honor of Rachel's good fortune, Victoria would have to sit it out. She has done nothing but complain all day about her sore toe. Perhaps she wants a little sympathy.

"I'm sorry about your toe, Victoria. It must hurt like the dickens."

"Mind your own business," she snapped.

"She deserves to be in pain," Lulu piped! "Just look what she did to my beautiful long ear."

"If your ear was less long and ugly it would not have gotten wedged between my teeth," Victoria snorted.

"Well ----it *is* a fact, Lulu. You do have lovely Landrace ears," Charlie said sweetly, breaking his silence.

He took me by surprise! "Do you honestly think Landrace ears are lovely Charlie?" I asked. "Do other hogs feel the same way?" I never thought of Landrace ears being anything but ugly, big elephant ears.

"Here we go again!" Elsie mocked. "Would someone tell Miss Super Pet about hogs and inform her that she should go back where she came from? Back to live with her *Mama and Papa!*"

"That's not nice, Elsie," Rachel said softly.

"You're right, Rachel," Charlie agreed.

Golly, just listen to this! Both Charlie *and* Rachel ----- showing me kindness. I thanked them politely. Elsie wouldn't dare talk back to Rachel. Not today, at least!

Dr. Pearson arrived with Papa. They headed for Rachel's pen.

"It's a miracle," he exclaimed. "Wouldn't have given you a nickel for her yesterday."

Papa had another job for the vet and that was to fix Victoria's toe. She started screaming before he even touched her. To safeguard his eardrums, he tied her mouth shut with a piece of rope until the job of putting a cast on her foot, was finished.

A peg stuck out the bottom of the cast for her to walk on. The new contraption looked funny, but I dare not laugh. Lulu laughed, boy, did she ever laugh! Charlie, Papa and Mama, they all laughed, but I thought I'd better not. At least, not until I turned my back. Then I did! So much, my belly ached.

Chapter 15.

WORK, A JOKE AND A TRAGEDY

TIME passed more quickly once I learned to make friends. By now, everybody in the building had heard about my "get well" message to Rachel. The story has been told so many times, by so may hogs, I'm not sure if it's still the same story.

The days became colder and shorter. Each day there was less sunlight. Winter zoomed in, all too soon. The front barn doors were shut most of the time now to keep out the cold and rain. Papa always sees to it that we have plenty of straw, some to lay on and some to sleep under.

Lately, when Mama comes to see me she brings a tiny white pig she calls "Peanuts". It's the scrawniest looking little fellow. The chances of it surviving are mighty slim. If the mother doesn't lie on it, the brothers and sisters will shove it away, so it will starve to

110

death. Twice a day, Mama brings it a bottle of warm milk. It reminds me of the way she took care of me, except I lived in the house. *My* mother didn't *want* me.

Speaking of mothers, the sows around me are good ones. Yet, when their pigs are weaned and are taken from them to the feeder building they show no sadness, only relief! I don't understand. When Hotsie and I are together again. I will ask her.

Today, Papa and Mama will get their exercise! It's moving day for a lot of weaner pigs. They pick them up, one at a time, tuck them gently in their arms and carry them to the feeder building.

Recently, a young man was hired to help move some pigs. The first thing he did was to pick one up by the hind legs. The poor thing began to squeal. Papa told him, "We don't do it that way, son. How would you like to travel face down with your feet in the air?"

The boy answered Papa by saying that *he* was not a pig and he and his dad always carried them that way and so does everybody else!

Papa took the noisy pig and lifted him gently to the lads arms. Then he gave the thankful porker a loving pat on the head.

About half way through the job I saw Papa's helper stop and read the sign on the front of the barn. The sign reads, ANYONE CAUGHT MOLESTING

MY HOGS WILL BE FOUND WITH HIS MOUTH
WIRED OPEN, BURIED IN THE FRESH MANURE
PILE. He gave the pig in his arms a loving pat, like he
had seen Papa do, and went on about his work.

Clementine played a bad joke on Mama and Papa.
For about two hours she kept them busy. The tricksy
old sow boiled from her gate with her pigs. Only the
pigs were supposed to come out. She headed for the
front barn door. It was open just enough for her to
make her escape. Papa was right behind her, calling
her back. But she kept on running, took off around
the barn.

Mama grabbed a bucket of feed and tried to coax
her in at the back door. For a minute it worked.

Clemmy snatched a mouthful of feed and then tore off around the other side of the building. She was having a holiday from her hog pen.

Papa chased her back around to the front door, which she passed, and continued on her merry-go-round.

Mama ran the opposite direction, hoping to head her off. With Papa behind her and Mama in front they managed to funnel her through the back door. Problem was, the front door was still open. The foxy old girl headed straight for it and out and around again.

Next time around they wised up and shut the barn doors behind her. Then all that was left was to get her through her gate.

By this time Mama and Papa were sucking in the air, but Clemmy didn't care at all. She chugged up and down the hallway enjoying her freedom. Papa decided to leave her alone. He said she'd go home when she got tired enough or thirsty. Shortly after, she did just that. Papa hurried in behind her and closed the gate.

Mama came in footsore and haggard. She sank to my straw, for a rest.

Papa was worn out too, but Blossom needed attention. Blossom was a Yorkshire sow due to have her pigs within the next few hours. With this cold weather, Papa wasn't taking any chances. He had already plugged in the heat lamp to make it toasty warm in the corner creep for the sow's pigs.

By late afternoon Papa and Mama went to the house, tired and hungry, knowing their day was not over yet!

A freezing wind howled and sent a bucket flying and rolling bumpity-bump ---across the frozen ground.

The night brought more disturbing noises. The wind had loosened a piece of metal roofing. It began to flap.

About midnight I felt an icy breeze when Mama and Papa opened the front door. Br-r-r! It was cold!

In a few minutes I heard Papa say, "She ate her supper and there's no milk in her nipples. She'll not be having those pigs until tomorrow." He had checked on Blossom.

I buried myself deeper in the straw to fortify against the burst of cold as they moved quickly through the door and on to the car.

Sometime later I was awakened again by that infernal loose roofing, pounding and popping.

For a moment the wind was silent. It was then I caught sound of something most fearful. I could hear the voices of new born babes and Blossom speaking to them as she shuffled restlessly re-arranging her bed.

How thoughtful Papa had been in putting the heat lamps on, in advance. Wise about the heat lamps but fooled by the sow's untimely delivery.

When morning came, Mama and Papa arrived bundled up like Eskimos! Papa said the thermometer on the outside of the barn read 12 below zero! That's cold! The coldest day I've ever seen!

Adult hogs require little heat. With the barn walls well insulated, thick wood planks for floors and all that wheat straw, we were quite comfortable.

I knew something Papa didn't. Blossom had delivered in the night. I watched as he looked into her pen. Quickly, he ran inside!

"What in the world?" he said. "She's having pigs already! What's the matter here? The little things didn't go to the heat! They're all piled up in another corner! Why I never saw anything like it! Pigs always go to heat!"

"Poor darlings!" Mama said, sadly. "I'll get them right into a hot tub, so they won't catch cold."

"Too late for that, Mama," Papa replied tearfully. "The poor little critters have froze to death."

Mama began to cry. I knew she would. I cried too. Other sows were crying. Even mean ol' Elsie.

"Come in and sit by the heat lamp, Mama. Stay here with Blossom. She's had eleven so far. There will likely be a few more." Papa said.

"We'll not lose the rest! That's for sure," Mama sobbed.

Blossom should have made sure those pigs went to the heat lamp. Perhaps she thought they did. I don't really know how hogs think. I suppose it's because I'm a 50-50.

A couple of hours later Mama came to see me. She had stopped crying.

"Blossom had bad luck, Priscilla. Eleven babies are dead, froze to death. Two more little girls were born about an hour ago. One has a snub nose like her mother. I named her Rosie. The other one has a long nose like her grandmother, Victoria. Papa named her Posey."

"It *was* a cold night, Mama. The coldest I've ever seen. I'm sorry for the sow," I said. "Are the new babies under the heat lamp?"

"You bet! They won't leave it --now that they've

found it," she said.

"Unless their mother calls them to eat," I remembered something Hotsie told me.

"Or when nature calls," she laughed. "You know Papa. Even though the pigs are safe, he will take up residence in that pen today."

"Yes. I know Papa. ----You say Victoria is a grandmother? Gol -------ly!"

I hope Rosie and Posey stay under the heat lamp!

Chapter 16.

A PIG, A POLICEMAN AND A BARBER SHOP

FRIEND Tom Cat strutted casually into my pen ---cocked his head to one side and gazed at me. I could detect a dramatic mood.

"Today," he said, "I have the power to grant you any wish! What will it be?"

"Oh! A game!" I said, pretending to play along. "Now let me see. My first wish, of course, would be to go home --back to the house. But, I know that is impossible. My second wish --to visit my friend, Hotsie."

With pretense of hat and cane, the silly cat tap danced somewhat of a soft shoe across my pen. He bowed a very low bow to me and said, "I am happy to announce --to-da --------YOUR WISH IS HEREBY GRANTED."

"I like your game, T.C., I wish it were for real."

"But it is --it is, my dear. Just a few minutes ago I overheard a conversation. *You* will soon be transported back across the orchard. It's off to the machine shed for you, where your old friend awaits your sweet presence."

"Then, this is all for real? It's not a game?" I asked.

"No way, Jose! *You* are going south. An older sow," he looked at me in a most peculiar way, "will be moving in here, in your pen."

How T.C. always manages to hear "big news" first has always puzzled me. No matter. The news was wonderful! He had made me happy.

"When, Tom Cat? When will they move me?" I asked.

"Could be in an hour or two," he replied.

"Good! Then we will have enough time to take care of an important matter. How do you feel about being Mr. Bright again?" I inquired.

"Ya mean deliver another one of those get well thingies?"

"That's what I mean. This time I want you to take it to Blossom," I told him. "Will you do it?"

"Of course! I find your tales most exuberating! You've been to some rather exciting places ---for a pig!" he chirped.

"I suppose I have," I agreed.

"I know Blossom is in good health and has two fine babies who love her, but losing eleven of her children must have left her very sad. You and I could cheer her up by sharing a funny incident that happened to me when Mama and Papa took me on that trip to California."

"Yes! Yes! I like this kind! Go ahead," he said, making himself comfortable.

"O.K., here goes. When we were on vacation, Papa stopped in Lawndale to see his old barber. That is a man who cuts hair," I said.

"I know, I know! Go on." He was anxious.

"When Papa and Mama went into the barber shop I was in the back seat of the car, asleep. When I woke up, I got a big surprise! I was in a parking lot of a gigantic shopping center. There were *millions* of cars and *billions* of people.

To get a better look at all of it, I jumped up to the top of the seat. Right away, some children saw me and began pecking on the window. They smiled and talked and pointed me out to passers-by. I had fun talking back to them.

More children crowded around. Parents came looking for their children and then they stayed.

Remember what I told you about the school children who never ever saw a pig in person?" T.C. nodded. "Well, these were city folks too. Likely, I was the first pig they had ever seen.

I was only a week old and loved all the attention. I ran around inside the car and rubbed my nose on the windows where they pecked. Good thing the car was locked. They would have petted me to pieces.

The crowd around the car grew to a mob and got loud. To get a better look at me, they began to push and shove each other.

Word reached the barber shop. There was a pig in a parked car out there that was causing quite a commotion. Papa told the folks in the barber shop, 'That's my car and Mama's pig!'

The barber asked Mama to go get the pig and bring it inside. She refused. He kept asking. Then he begged, like a kid. Mama finally agreed to come and get me, just to shut him up.

She had a hard time getting to the car until the people saw she had keys in her hand. Then they made a path and began to clamor for favors! Just like those school kids! 'Let me hold the pig' and 'I wanna pet the pig'.

The crowd continued to grow. Things really got jammed up good. Nobody could get in or out of the parking lot.

Mama jumped inside and locked the door. She began to laugh. A police officer stepped up to the car.

'What's the problem here?' he asked.

About six dozen kids told him about me, all at the same time. I was standing on Mama's shoulder in

the car. The policeman saw me and forgot his job. *He*
wanted to hold me too. Can you believe that? Mama
was about to split her sides. She rolled down the car
window, just a sliver.

'Give me safe escort to the barber shop and I'll
let you carry Priscilla.' Mama's laughter had turned in
to a silly cackle so that big tears were gushing down
her face and splashing on her hands.

'Come on,' said the officer. He looked at Mama
and then, he began to laugh. It *was* funny.

We headed for the barber shop. Mama held on to
the policeman and he held on to me.

A redheaded boy with gooey chocolate on his
face, ran after us and grabbed at me. 'Don't let him
touch me,' I squealed. So they ran a little faster.

When we reached the barber shop, Mama took
me and hurried through the door. The policeman told
the people to get back in their cars and decongest the
area.

Papa, the barber, and some other men had been
watching us from the large front window. Papa said if
he had known it was so much fun to bring a pig on
vacation he would have done it before.

In the barber shop, I had fun running all over
the place. The barber would throw hair on me and I
would shake it off. He gave me a drink of water from
a shaving mug. While I drank, he took my picture.

When we left there the people had gone. I guess

they had gone decongesting. But no matter, another batch of folks began to gather as we passed by the stores on our way to the car.

I heard a woman say, 'What a peculiar looking dog.'

Then we passed a hot dog stand. A man and his boy were sitting on stools eating. When the man spotted me, he spun around so fast that he knocked his boy to the floor."

Tom Cat had constrained himself for as long as he could. Now, he literally rolled with laughter! Someone else laughed too, I thought as I continued.

"Mama and Papa took off running to the car. Then, there he was again. That same cop. Standing by the car.

'Figured you would need some help getting out of the parking lot,' he said.

'You figure pretty good,' Papa told him.

'Next time you folks come to Lawndale, let me know ahead of time,' he said, 'I'll arrange a special honor guard for you and your pig and notify the television station.' He waved a friendly good-bye to us and moved the people back so we could get away.

"Well, that's it," I said. "Can you remember all that for Blossom?"

"No need!" T.C. answered. "Look!"

I looked around. Charlie and all the sows near enough to hear us were on their feet, listening to the story.

"If your story was a 'get well message' to cheer me ----it worked," Blossom said. "Thank you for sharing it with us."

"I loved the story. Tonight I'll dream of far away places, places I've never been," said a sweet little voice. I think it was Carlotta.

"Is the story true?" Lulu asked.

"Every word," I told her.

"Impossible! I don't believe a word of it!" Elsie mumbled.

"Sorry, Luv," Tom Cat said to Elsie, "if the story was a bit over you head!"

Tom Cat was being unkind.

Actually, the story may have been too hard for her to understand. But why didn't she believe me?

Chapter 17.

MABEL

PAPA sauntered through the barn door with a Landrace sow. Well advanced in years she was, and time worn. She limped along as if in pain.

"Priscilla, do you remember your mother?" Papa asked.

My *mother*? Don't tell me *this* is my mother?

Mama arrived, giving out terrible advice. "Let's put Mabel in with Priscilla for a few hours. They'll get along together -----I think!"

What? How could Mama do this to me? I don't want that old sow in here! She tried to squash me once, almost killed me! She might try it again. I'd be dead right now if it weren't for Mama and Papa! No sir! I don't want her in here with me!

Like it or not, Papa threw open my gate and in she came.

125

"Get her out of here," I shouted! "Get her out! I don't want her in here!" T.C. hurried down to get a closer look.

"Priscilla, give her a chance! She's not so bad! And don't yell, it doesn't become you," Tom Cat pleaded.

"Mama, how could you do this to me? Get this old hog out of here!" I begged.

"Priscilla! Darling! Where are your manners? Of all the people in the world you should respect your mother ----more than anyone else!" Mama said.

"She's *not* my mother! She's not! She's just an old hog!"

"Listen to that!" Elsie jeered. "What did I tell you? Little Miss Super Pet thinks she's a person!"

"Well, maybe I am," I said, then turned and walked away and lay down on my straw with my back to the cussed old thing!

"You'll just have to trust my decision this time, Priscilla," Mama said as she walked away.

I was beaten, penned up with a killer sow. My friends had forsaken me. Mama and Papa left, and the Tom Cat was doing what he does best, sitting up above me, passing out judgment. He might as well be God!

"How are you Mabel?" Charlie asked.

"Not too bad, Charlie, for my age," she said. "My legs torment me some, in this cold weather."

"Your daughter there, she's a lot like you Mabel," he continued. "I suppose you've heard about her special talent for cheering up the sick?"

"Yes! I've heard that her stories are very good," she replied.

I jumped to my feet! "What have you heard?" I snapped. "Who would tell *you* anything about *me?*"

"Almost everyone, child," she answered. "Now I know you don't like me, that's obvious and you have every right to your opinion ......"

"You bet I do!" I shouted. "You lay on me! If it weren't for Papa and Mama, I'd be dead."

"Every word is true, child," she said sadly.

"And *don't call me 'Child'*, I yelled at her, *I am not your child*. You threw me out! Admit it! Didn't you throw me out?"

Mabel began to cry, bitterly. I was showing her! I was finally getting even!

"Priscilla," Charlie roared. "How could you be so cruel? I am astonished at your cold hearted abuse of your mother! Do you know who you sound like now, Priscilla? Elsie, that's who! But you, my Priscilla ------ This does not sound like you."

Scrud! Now he's rooting at the same tune as the Tom Cat! Charlie's defense for Mabel went on and on. A real lecture. It began to bore me!

"Are you through talking?" I said to Charlie, "I don't want to hear another word of this!"

"No, I am *not* through. There's more. And it's about time you heard the whole story!" he insisted. "I'd say you're old enough now to understand. So, you just listen for a minute!"

What could I say? I had no choice. I was penned in.

"One day a vicious dog showed up in the pasture, looking for trouble," Charlie began. "Several sows were out there grazing. They saw the dog and tried to run for safety but their speed was no match for his. Mabel was heavy with pigs. It was difficult for her to run. She trailed to the rear of the other sows. The dog caught up to her first.

"He sank his teeth into her legs again and again, tearing the flesh. His teeth were razor sharp and jagged. Mabel fought back bravely.

"The Mr. heard the commotion. He grabbed a stick and chased the dog away. But the damage was done. Mabel's legs were ripped open. Her bones were showing and blood was spurting out.

"Mabel was put in that very pen. Dr. Pearson came to sew up her cuts. He worked for hours! That night, she had her babies, unexpectedly. You, Priscilla, were in that litter. You were the last one born."

"No," Mabel said. "She was next to the last." Mabel was still crying.

"So you see, Priscilla, your mother was in a bad way when you were born," Charlie added.

"I am not totally heartless, you know. I'm sorry Mabel was bitten. But I don't know what all this has to do with me," I said.

"Well, I'll tell you! After her pigs were all born, Mabel got up to straighten her bed. It was all she could do to stand on her sore legs. When she lay down, you ran right under her!" Charlie explained.

"I tried and tried to get up," Mabel sobbed, "but my legs were too weak."

"Fortunately, your mother was able to raise a shoulder, just enough for one of your brothers to root you out of the way," Charlie said. "And that's when the Mr. and Mrs. found you nearly lifeless, in the pen."

I remember something like that happening to me. I thought it was a dream. Maybe I had been wrong about Mabel, and yet, there was another incident that bothered me.

"But Mama tried to give me back to you after *she* had made me well. *That,* I remember! *You* didn't want me!" I was still being hateful.

"You *were* healthy and doing just fine, but any one of my other children would have made two of you, Priscilla. Your brothers and sisters would have pushed you back. I'm sorry, Priscilla, but you would have starved to death," she said sadly. "I knew if the Mr. and Mrs. raised you, your chances of survival would be much better. It was hard to give you up, a great sacrifice. But I loved you enough to push you back to your Mama. It was a day I shall never forget."

"Neither will I," I told her. "Mama told me what Papa said. He said, 'Pick up your baby Mama and let's go,' so she picked me up, took me to the house and raised me."

"Do you understand now, Priscilla?" she asked.

"Yes," was all I could say. I cried and so did my mother.

"I'm glad we've had this time together," she said.

"I wish I hadn't said those bad things to you," I said. "I really meant them, but I know better now."

"You are beginning to sound like your old self again, Priscilla," Charlie said.

"Stop humoring the little beast," Elsie said hotly.

"Hush, Elsie!" Mabel commanded. "I want you to behave yourself." Elsie quieted down immediately.

"Gosh! You sure have a way with Elsie! Nobody else can make her behave. She's a mean one, you know," I told mother.

"Not really so mean, Priscilla. She's just jealous of you. You went to the house, she went to the barn. You slept on a soft bed and looked at television. She has never seen a soft bed or a television. You went on a trip to California. Elsie has never been off the farm."

"I don't understand, Mother," I was puzzled. "Why should she be jealous of *me?*"

"Why child, -----------------didn't you know? Elsie is your sister." she said.

"My sister? Elsie?"

Chapter 18.

MOTHERS TO BE

MAMA looked curiously happy when she saw how well Mabel and I were getting along together. I had doubts about it but I don't think Mama ever did.

When evening came I was moved back to the machine shed. Not having to share the pen, Mother would have more room. As for me, I was dying to see Hotsie!

As soon as my gate swung open, I darted out and hightailed it across the orchard.

Hotsie was not in the yard. There was the familiar little green gate. I waited for Mama to open it. Then I hurried through the yard and peeked into the opened door of the building.

They she lay, asleep on the straw. Looking wonderful! Much improved over the last time I saw her. Perhaps the privacy of the machine shed, and of

133

course, Papa's care, had done the job.

She began to stir. Suddenly, she saw me and quickly but gracefully, lifted herself to her feet.

"Little One!" she said, in her lovely voice. "You are home. We can be together once again! My goodness, Priscilla! Just look at you! More beautiful than ever!"

Me? Beautiful? I had never thought of myself as ------------beautiful! Mama says I am, but I thought she just said it because she loves me. I'll think about that later. But right now I have something special to share.

"Hotsie, I've kept my secret long enough. I wanted you to be the first to hear the news!"

"What is it?" she asked anxiously.

"*I am going to be a mother,* Hotsie! Me! Priscilla! I am going to be a mother!" I said.

"How wonderful! That *is* good news!" she said. Then looking at me squarely, she probed. "Is there other news. Little One?"

"You mean about my mother?"

"Yes. That's what I mean." She smiled.

"How did you know?" I asked.

"The Tom Cat knows everything." She laughed.

"Did he tell you how dreadful I treated poor Mabel when Papa and Mama put her in my pen?" I asked.

"Yes, he did. T.C. 'tells' everything, you know." We both laughed. "I always knew you could work it out with your mother if you were given the opportunity to talk to her. Mabel is one of my favorites. When you lived in the house, she kept track of you the best she could. I've seen her watch for hours for the Mr. and Mrs. to drive up to the barn, hoping you would be in the car and she could catch a glimpse of you."

I had no idea.

"Knowing the truth about her after all this time makes me feel good all over. Mama must have known how I use to feel about Mabel. I don't know how she knew, but she's the one who put Mabel in my pen."

"I hear other things about you too, Little One. A good many of the sows are your friends now. You've won them over. Just like I knew you would. Remember when you were afraid no one would like you?" she asked.

"I remember. But Hotsie, they don't all like me. Elsie hates me!" I told her, "and she's my sister!"

"I've heard about Elsie. Be patient, Priscilla. You'll win her for a friend, yet." Hotsie sounded positive. For the first time, since I've known Hotsie, I didn't believe her. Elsie will never like me.

The last sunrays of the evening streaked across our pen. As Hotsie ambled through them, her coat glistened like thousands of diamonds. Each hair had a little droplet of oil clinging to it, thanks to Papa. He sure looks out for his Hotsie. *She* gets brushed with *clear* oil to keep her coat pure white. Papa takes a lot of pride in her beauty. She is *the most beautiful sow* I have ever seen.

One day, while I lived in the farrowing barn, Papa brought in a sow that looked a lot like Hotsie. But she was younger. She held her head erect and moved with charm and grace like Hotsie does.

Charlie caught me staring at the young sow. *He was looking at her too.* "Bet you thought it was Hotsie!" he said.

I had to admit, I did at first. Charlie told me her name was Peaches. Hotsie's daughter. I was not surprised! But ask me if I was impressed. I was!

Hotsie is expecting her 8th litter of pigs. Under the circumstances, conditions for her were perfectly normal. My condition was another matter. I was not quite sure how I was supposed to feel.

The days were pleasant and passed quickly. My friend and I ate and slept and talked, then ate and slept and talked some more. Sunny days became more frequent. Afternoons, we lay out in the yard.

My favorite lying down spot was not the same. I didn't fit it any more. Since I last lived here, I had put on about fifty pounds and was gaining every day. Hotsie grew faster than I. Maybe it's because she's older, and much larger, to start with.

Another thing bothered me. Much of the time I felt miserable and sick. Sometimes, in the night, I felt like the barn was spinning. I dared not mention it to anyone. I didn't want to be troublesome.

"They are gaining too fast!" Papa said one evening as he checked our feed box. "But aren't they gorgeous? Did you ever see a better looking pair of hogs?"

"No, I never did," Mama answered as she added more fresh water to the big rubber tub. "I'm anxious to see what Priscilla's pigs look like. I hope they all look like her!" She smiled at me.

"They're both due in June. Toward the last of the month. Priscilla should have her pigs on the 23rd and Hotsie on the 27th," Papa said, checking the calender.

"That's good. Then they'll be in the farrowing barn at the same time. You'll like that, won't you girls?" Mama asked. "My Priscilla is a big girl now, Papa. It's hard to believe that she was born just last February."

Papa had finished brushing Hotsie. Now, I would get me turn. "Priscilla got along good with Mabel, after she settled down," he said.

"They had to have their time together. I knew they'd get along. Priscilla needed to get to know her mother," Mama said.

Papa scratched his head. "You and that pig! I never tell anybody about you and Priscilla talking to each other. I'm afraid folks would think that ya don't have both yer paddles in the water, Mama."

Mama just laughed at him. "I don't care what anybody says!" she said. But Papa knew that already.

Chapter 19.

THE DAY I DID SOMETHING BAD

TOM CAT popped in with an interesting bit of news. "Victoria feels slighted," he announced.

"Victoria? What ever for?" I asked.

"The old girl is feeling sorry for herself. Hasn't been much excitement in her life lately. Not since she stopped jumping fences, biting ears, bustin' toes, etc., etc., etc., --Yeah! She's very upset with you, Priscilla!"

"With me?" I asked.

"Yes! With you! She told me you were her nearest neighbor when she broke her toe. And no matter how much she moaned and groaned *you* never once offered *her* one of your get well stories."

"So-o, the tired old warrior wants to hear a story, huh?" It had never occurred to me that Victoria needed cheering. Perhaps I did slight her.

139

"Well, Tom Cat, if Victoria wants a story, let's give her one. Alright?" I asked. I knew just the tale for her.

"Alright." He made himself comfortable.

Hotsie came closer. "I've only heard these stories second hand. Now I'll get to hear it from you, Priscilla."

"One day when Papa was cleaning pens," I began, "Don Lounsbury came to visit. While Papa cleaned, he sat on the top boards of the pens and watched and visited.

"Victoria's cast had just been removed. Papa had turned her out in the pasture to get some exercise. So, Victoria was not in the barn and did not see what I am about to tell you.

"This visitor was Papa's friend and he knew how much Papa thought of his hogs. He started teasing Papa a little bit.

"He read aloud the sign in the barn which said, ANYONE CAUGHT MOLESTING THESE HOGS WILL BE FOUND WITH HIS MOUTH WIRED OPEN, BURIED ALIVE, IN THE MANURE PILE.

" 'That's a funny sign,' he said to Papa.

" 'Not meant to be funny,' Papa said. 'Just don't want anybody messin' with my hogs.'

"While Papa cleaned Victoria's pen. He peered down at me. I was resting on my straw.

" 'Is this the pig you guys raised in the house?' he asked, pointing to my name plate. 'Wasn't she a Priscilla?'

" 'That's her, the same little girl -----all grown up.' Papa smiled as he carried in an armload of straw.

" 'When ya gonna eat her?' the visitor asked.

" 'We never will,' Papa snapped.

"Eat her? Eat her? How dare he sit on my pen and ask such a terrible thing! I got up, bounced right over to where he was sitting and *bit him* right in the butt! Not too hard. But hard enough, so he could feel it.

"He let out a yell.

" 'She bit me,' he said with a surprised look on

his face. 'She bit me,' he repeated, as he jumped down off my pen.

" 'Serves you right,' Papa said. 'You should never have said what you did! We don't eat our hogs! We raise them up to be good pig producers, --------brood sows. No. Priscilla wouldn't stand for you sayin' a thing like that. Eating Priscilla would be like eating a member of the family!' Papa stopped working and looked squarely at his friend. He had a smile on his face and his hands on his hips.

" 'Didn't bite ya hard, did she?'

" 'No! But I felt it!' he answered. 'How did that pig know what I said?'

" 'She's smart, that one. She's been to school!' Papa went on about his business."

As usual the Tom Cat laughed and rolled and laughed some more.

"Did that actually happen, Priscilla?" Hotsie chuckled. "Did you bite that man?"

"I sure did," I answered. "Do you think Victoria will like the story, Tom Cat?" I chose this one for her because it had a little violence in it.

He clawed to the top board snickering all the while. "She'll love it!" he said. With one forceful lunge he was out of sight.

I've often wondered how he tells the stories. Maybe, someday, I'll find out.

Chapter 20.

THE WAITING IS ALMOST OVER

THE machine shed was a peaceful place to live. Hotsie and I were quite content. Often, I think of Mabel and Charlie and now and then, one of the others.

Tom Cat is always good for news from the far-rowing barn. Since I last saw my mother, she has had another litter of thirteen pigs and weaned them already! Please God! Let none of them be like Elsie!

Mama came in with her apron full of apples. I wonder where she got them. So far, our apple trees have produced only blossoms.

She sat down on a bail of straw and put her head back to rest. "It's more quiet than usual," she said.

"No wonder! We have no music! T.C. chased the neighbors cat in behind our radio and the two of them sent it sailing off the shelf!" I told her.

Mama got up to investigate. She picked up the

radio, put it back on the shelf and plugged it in. It worked! We didn't get to enjoy it for long.

Two days later Hotsie and I were moved to the farrowing barn. I had come to love living in the machine shed and dreaded leaving it. I wish Hotsie and I could stay right there and have our babies. I asked Mama about it but she said there just wasn't enough room for two families.

The air was crisp and sweet as we trotted through the orchard. Noisy birds flew from tree to tree watching our every move. Mitzi ran ahead and Papa plugged along behind, whistling a cheerful little tune.

I tried my best to enjoy the occasion and freedom of being "out"! But how can you enjoy anything when you feel bad? Wouldn't you know it? Just when the opportunity comes for me to run around and get some exercise, all I feel like doing is putting one foot ahead of the other!

Hotsie seemed in the best of spirits. As she loped merrily along, her bottles clinked! If you know what I mean!

"I'll be glad when the apples are ripe," she said. "I believe I love apples more than anything else there is to eat. I like red ones, green ones, yellow ones, halves, pieces, sauce, rinds and any other way apples can be eaten!"

At least Hotsie was feeling good and that made me happy.

"I've been in this orchard many times, Little One," she said. "But today, because you are with me, it's a special occasion."

"Thank you, Hotsie. You are indeed my very best friend." I told her.

Hotsie and I were placed side by side in the barn. The front pen was again my home. Hotsie was given the pen next to me. Charlie and Mabel had occupied these two pens but they were nowhere in sight.

"Won't be long now!" Mama said as she rubbed my neck. "Better get all the rest you can ---while you can get it. When those babies of yours arrive you'll have your hands full. I hope at least one of your baby girls look like you. I've got a name picked out already! 'Little Prissy'! That's kind of short for Priscilla. Papa is betting you have 10 pigs. I think 8 would be plenty for the first time. In a couple more days we will know for sure, won't we?" Mama was anxious about my babies, so anxious she fussed over me to see that everything was just so. And all the while she fussed, she smiled, and kept up a one-sided conversation.

Papa put fresh water in our drinking tubs and then, they left us.

I looked for a familiar face but couldn't find one. However, these sows knew us! I heard them talking! Someone said, "The queen is back. Priscilla is with her." Then I overheard something about "her 8th litter" and "105 pigs".

Hotsie was arranging her straw.

"Hotsie," I whispered. "Psst -------Hotsie, are they talking about you? *Have you had 105 pigs?*"

"Yes, Little One, 105 babies. I'm always afraid I'll have a smaller litter and dissappoint the Mr. He calls me his 'queen' you know, and he brags on me so. It's expected of me to have a lot of babies. So far, I have." She began to cry. "Wouldn't it be terrible if ----------?"

"Don't worry, Hotsie!" Seeing her cry upset me terribly. "You'll have a big litter. I know you will. And Hotsie, I know Papa too! Why, even if you didn't have a lot of pigs, you'd still be his queen. I can tell. *You* are *his* favorite, just as I am Mama's"

Quickly, I changed the subject.

"Do you know any of these hogs around here? I don't know a single one. Wonder where Charlie and Mabel are?"

"They could be down at the other end of the building," she answered, between sobs. "Before we leave here again, you'll see many of your old friends."

"I'm sure you're right, Hotsie. Who is this young sow across from me?" I asked, determined to keep her from thinking about herself. "She looks like she's taking a nap."

"Yes. I know her. She's Hattie, and this is her first time in the farrowing barn. Her mother's name is

Peaches."

I definitely remember Peaches. She is the beautiful sow I mistook one day for Hotsie.

"Then this sow -------then Hattie is your granddaughter?" How strange! Hotsie, a grandmother. She certainly doesn't seem like a grandmother. *People* grandmothers are sometimes old and wrinkled, but Hotsie is beautiful and quite youthful.

"Is that so hard for you to believe, Little One?" she asked.

I dared not answer for fear of saying the wrong thing. The thought had not occurred to me before. Never have I heard a sow speak of her grandchildren. Only a few of them ever have anything to say about their own children. How strange! When I am old and have grandchildren, I shall love and revere them. And, I will fuss over each little fellow, just the way Mama fusses over me.

I felt very tired. I think Hotsie did too. We each went our seperate ways, to rest. For some reason I felt not only weary, but dejected.

Chapter 21.

DISAPPOINTMENT

TWO hours later I was still feeling strange and alone. I wished for Mama. Why couldn't she be here when I wanted her?

T.C. was last seen with two of his lady friends----- racing out the door. I noticed he was smiling, a lot!

Oh dear! Why can't I get comfortable? I wished for my radio. I walked around and around my pen. The floor creaked. Probably always had, but I never paid any attention to it, until now! The barn began to spin! Where was Mama? Feeling very foolish, I began to cry. Just a little at first, but a little didn't seem to be enough. I wept in silence.

The goats sauntered idly by the barn door and gawked at me with long knowing glances. Papa was on their heels and Mama on his.

"Mama! Mama!" I whispered huskily.

She heard me. And I was relieved.

Quietly, she reached for my brush and brushed me with calm caresses. Soon I relaxed enough to go about my work. I rearranged my straw for comfort. Papa looked in and smiled at me and at Mama.

"Are you going to stay with her?" he asked.

"As long as she needs me," Mama answered. Papa would have been surprised if she had said anything else. For that matter, so would I!

"How much longer do you think it will be?" he inquired.

"I'd say, sometime after supper. If she drops off to sleep I'll go in the house and get a sandwich." Mama sat down by my head in the straw.

I wanted Mama there, and yet I didn't want to talk. My head was still spinning like a six gun. I'd keep my problem to myself. I didn't want to be troublesome.

Sometimes the smallest bunch of straw out of place in a bed can inflict sheer torture.

"I have to re-do my bed," I told Mama. I jumped right up to get it done.

"Move slowly. Save yourself," Mama advised. "But get it done and lie back down."

No one else took notice of my predicament, except Hotsie who occasionally opened her eyes and looked toward me, but said nothing. When she saw me up, she broke her silence.

"Do as your Mama told you, Priscilla. Do not tire

yourself. Hurry with what you are doing and lie back down."

"My bed was uncomfortable. It felt like it had a football in it!" I explained.

"Your bed will be uncomfortable many times before this night has ended. Wait as long as you can each time before getting up to remake it. Lie down, Little One, and talk to us about some of the happy times you have had." My friend was the voice of experience.

"Thank you dear Hotsie," I said to her before tucking in the last piece of straw.

On a sudden impulse I slipped over by the gate where a clean pile of straw lay in a bunch. I gathered some up in my mouth, took it to Mama and dropped it in her lap. She caught her breath and dipped to one side. I guess she thought I was going to step on her. I would never do that! What I had in mind, if she didn't push the straw off her lap, was to use it for a pillow.

"Taking advantage of a situation, aren't you?" Mama chuckled.

I didn't answer, but settled down again on my bed. This time I managed to get part of my head on Mama's lap. Just my head weighs more now than all of me weighed when I was a baby. I didn't want to squash Mama! Luckily, she didn't push me off.

"I'm glad you are here, Mama," I said.

"Me too," she replied.

"I'm glad *you* are near, Hotsie."

"I'm glad too, Little One," she answered ----between yawns.

How wonderful to have family and friends around me to share in this great occasion. Imagine! Me, Priscilla, with my very own pigs ----soon to arrive.

"How is your memory, Priscilla?" Mama asked.

"Excellent! I can remember everything, from the moment I was born."

"You can, huh? Let's see. Do you remember when I carried you into the house for the first time?" she asked.

"Well, ----------gosh, no! Why can't I remember?"

That's odd, I thought. "I do remember waking up in the big bed between you and Papa."

"The reason you can't remember is because you were unconscious. When your mother lay on you --"

"She didn't mean to," I quickly reminded her.

"Of course she didn't *mean* to, Priscilla! Now, getting back to my story, you were unconscious for a long time. When I picked you up from the pen I thought sure you were a goner! Good thing you twitched a little bit or I would have dug a hole and buried you in it."

"Oh! Mama! Don't say such things!"

"Sorry. For two and a half days you didn't open your eyes. We kept you wrapped up in an enormous white bath towel to keep you warm. It was in the winter time, you know. Papa tucked you in bed between us at night. We took turns getting up every two hours to feed you a few drops of goat milk."

"Which goat's milk did I get?" I asked, remembering the argument between Gertie and Patches.

"Both, I imagine. I just mix it all up together," she said.

I had to laugh in spite of my condition. "I must remember to tell the nannies."

While I had an off and on nap Mama managed to wiggle out from under my head. When I awoke she was there munching on some cookies and drinking a soda pop.

All was silent. And then, the waiting was over! The first baby pig was born, and then another. Papa came to help.

"What's the matter here?" Papa cried. The infants made no sound! None! They were lifeless! They did not wiggle or squeal or jump about like new born pigs are supposed to.

More and more babies were born, one after the other. I watched breathlessly for some sign of life, an ear to twitch, a tail to flick, an eye to blink. Something! Anything!

It was more than I could bear! My babies were all being born dead! I felt cold and helpless! I wanted to die.. I was a complete failure! There would be no trophy for *me!* Papa would never call *me* a queen! Life had dealt me a painful blow!

"My babies! My babies!" I cried.

Large tears streamed down Mama's face and splashed where they dropped.

Papa wept when he saw Mama's grief.

Dr. Pearson was sent for. He was a quiet, gentle man, old for his age and very wise.

"Isn't this the sow that was crushed when it was a baby?" he asked.

"Just a tiny baby when it happened!" Papa said sadly.

Dr. Pearson shook his head. "I know how much you love this little sow," he said to Mama. "I would not breed her anymore. Another litter might kill her! I don't think you want that to happen!"

What? No more litters? I'll *never* get to be a mother! Papa will *sell* me for sure! I'm no good for anything.

Papa picked up my nine little dead babies and put them in a cardboard box. He put the box gently under his arm and left with the doctor.

Mama stayed. "Don't cry my Priscilla," she blubbered. "You aren't the first sow to lose an entire litter and you won't be the last. It wasn't your fault. You couldn't help it. It just happens sometimes."

"But my babies! I've waited so long for them to be born! Now they're gone and I'll never see them again," I cried.

Hotsie tried to comfort me. "Life is cruel sometimes, Little One. But you are very courageous. You have already faced many more problems than most sows have to face. And now my friend, you must try to forget this night as quickly as you can."

"Forget? Forget? I will never forget!" I sobbed.

"You must," she gently commanded.

The awful truth struck me. "How can I ever show my face again -----to anyone?"

"Priscilla," Hotsie said, "Have you forgotten Rachel? She lost all but Carl and Carlotta. Then there was Blossom. Her pigs froze to death!"

"But Hotsie, Blossom and Rachel each had two

pigs that lived. I've got nothing, not even one!" I cried even harder.

For a long time they both tried to console me. I knew they meant well, but it was no use, I would not be consoled.

So close to good fortune! This time I almost reached my mountain top! The darkness of the night seemed to swallow me up.

High in the rafters above my pen sat a silent friend, alone with his grief for my misfortune. How long had he been there? I wondered.

After some time had passed, Mama and Papa gave me a hug and a promise to return when it was daylight.

I cried myself to sleep.

Chapter 22.

MY LUCKY NUMBER

GRIEF is a word that you need to feel to know its meaning. Tonight, I learned the true, horrid meaning. The feeling of a great injustice. The mental pain.

I also learned that sleep does not come easily when one grieves. I stared into the darkness and thought of my beautiful babies, gone forever.

Then suddenly, without warning, another pig was born! My nightmare was not over. There it was, another baby.

Papa was not here to take this one away. At least I could keep it for a while. Even if it's dead, it belongs to me! I suppose it's dead, I thought, taking a closer look.

Whoa! What's this? I think it moved! I'm *sure* it moved! Can I believe what I'm seeing? Its *eyes* are open! It blinked! It's alive! It really *is* alive! The pig

157

began to jump about making pleasant noises. His little voice was the most beautiful sound I had ever heard. Better than sleigh bells and banjo pickin'.

"Oh, baby!" I yelled at the top of my lungs. "I'm a mother! *I have a pig! An alive pig!*" Ask me if I care if I wake up every hog in the place. Just ask me if I care! I don't care at all. I *had* to tell someone. I had to announce the good news!

"Hotsie! Hotsie! Wake up! Somebody! *Everybody!*" I shouted. "I have a baby. It wiggles! It jumps! It blinks its eyes and flicks its ears! It's alive! Everybody, it's alive!" I cried. I just could not shut up. "Tom Cat, are you up there? Mother, Charlie, everybody, listen to me."

"We *are* listening," Hotsie shouted with joyful voice. "How can we avoid it?" She laughed. "Congratulations, Little One! I am truly happy that you have a baby of your own."

"Yes, Priscilla, congratulations indeed are in order," someone said. And there were other kind regards from the sows. *None* of them was the least bit hateful.

"Talk to your son," Hotsie advised. "You and I can talk in the morning," she yawned.

"Good idea," I answered, feeling exceedingly chipper. "I want to get acquainted with him anyway. Whoops?? Just a minute! I think it's ---yeah, it is! It's a little girl!"

All who could hear me, laughed. I felt good, knowing the sows were happy at my good fortune.

One pig! One is my lucky number. Just when I was feeling sorry for myself, knowing full well I can never have another litter of pigs, this wonderful thing happened to me. Thank you God, I thought, and cried a little.

The newborn lost no time in finding her place to eat. So many choice spots for one little girl. She was, oh so pretty! Rusty red all over. There was no wide white belt nor white on her legs like me, just rusty red ------all over. Rusty red was going to be my favorite color from now on.

The pig looked healthy and strong. All she has

done so far, is eat and look satisfied!

Oh! Won't Mama and Papa be surprised!

Where is that cat? He's gone from the rafters!

"T.C." I yelled, getting numerous complaints. I forgot! I'm wide awake and everybody else is trying to sleep!

Tom Cat slithered through the boards in my pen----panting and out of breath.

"Priscilla, was that *you* yelling? Are you all right?" he asked.

I was lying in the darkest corner of my pen with my baby. T.C. did not suspect there was another pig. His concern was for me. He came nearer and spied the little creature. He stopped short on all fours.

"Look!" I said proudly.

He sat there gaping and blinked back a tear. The pig had gone to sleep but was still holding on to lunch. T.C. gave the baby a gently lick on the face, then sat down about a foot away, wrapped his tail about himself and just looked.

"One is all you need, Priscilla, when the one is as perfect and lovely as she is," Tom Cat told me. That was nice, I thought.

"Thank you, my friend. She is lovely, isn't she? Mama wanted to name *one* of my daughters 'Little Prissy'. It's kind of short for Priscilla, I think."

"How come your Mama and Papa left?" he asked.

"They thought all my babies had been born.

Mama would never have left me if she thought there would be more," I assured him. "You know, Tom Cat, this one little baby will help me forget my sorrow for all the others who did not live. This one little pig, ------I do love it so."

It had been a long night and I was tired. I closed my eyes.

"You sleep. I'll baby sit the little porker." Tom Cat sat and watched.

I had one last look to make sure Little Prissy was for real. Then I slept.

Chapter 23.

HAPPY DREAMS

NOW that I have a family, my house will be a home. I am the lady of the house and after a hard day's work have earned the luxury of a baby sitter.

As I closed my eyes, a mysterious blanket of peace covered me. Again, I opened one eye to steal a last peek at my little girl. She was there all right. She was real. And best of all, she belonged to me.

There was something mystic, supernatural about the way I felt. I knew I would dream wonderful dreams of my happy childhood.

Very soon I drifted away to my soft pillow by Mama's and Papa's bed. Visions of that unforgettable vacation trip filled my head.

In my dreams I relived our visit to Las Vegas, Nevada, the city of bright lights and gambling casinos. My parents had tickets to a Johnny Mathis concert.

162

Mama loves to hear him sing.

We had not made hotel reservations. Papa said with me along they would have to look for an out of the way motel, and sneak me in. He made me feel tertible.

Mama disagreed. "I'm not going to spend the night in some big city dump," she said. "And I'll not allow you or Priscilla to do it either! I've always heard that 'anything goes' in Las Vegas. So, let's give it a try."

A few minutes later we pranced right in to the lobby of one of the finest hotels the city had to offer and headed for the desk to register for a room. In fact, Mama and Papa strutted around like they owned the place.

I was tucked neatly under Mama's arm. In plain sight. But no one, I mean -----no one, paid any attention to me!

The hotel was different from any other place I'd been! The people kept right on doing what they were doing! And I wasn't too sure what that was!

The hotel lights were as dim as daytime in the potato cellar. Crazy place, this Las Vegas! The streets are beautifully bright, lights everywhere. But where are the people? Not outside, enjoying the lights! The people are inside, stumbling around in the dark, putting their money in metal boxes, breathing air that smells like someone set fire to a manure pile and sipping on drinks as foul as soured hog mash.

A man's voice on the loud speaker said, "Fifty dollar jackpot on number 204." I thought it would be nice to win fifty dollars but the lady at machine number 204 didn't crack a smile when she collected her money. I asked Mama why. She said that lady had probably put more than fifty dollars into that machine already. That's dumb, I thought.

It looks like they put money in the box and pull on a crank to get it out again. It just doesn't make any sense! And where are all the children? Could it be that they are smarter about money than adults?

Papa signed the register. A young man wearing a red suit with gold buttons came toward us. He had a great suntan.

"Let me take your dog to the kennel," he said.

Mama grinned. "No, thank you. I'll just keep her with me. She's part of my act and we need to rehearse."

What on earth was Mama talking about! Papa winked at Mama. I could see they were having a good time. And if they were, I was too.

"All right ma'm," the fellow said to Mama.

The truth was out! In all the excitement of this dark place, no one had noticed that I was a pig.

Next, we got into the elevator. It stopped before we got up to our floor. A drunk got on. I knew he was drunk. I've seen drunks on television.

He stared at me and rocked around like a palsied pea-cock. He slapped playfully at me. I didn't like it! Besides, he smelled terrible. Finally, he got a little too close with his slapping. So, I bit his finger. Not too hard, but hard enough so he'd keep his hands to himself.

"You are a naughty pussy cat!" he croaked in his whisky voice. Well now! I had never, ever been mistaken for a cat. We left the elevator laughing. The drunk was still in there with a silly look on his face.

My dreams left Las Vegas and wandered on to another pleasant time in my youth.

I dreamed I was at home and the telephone was ringing.

The phone sat on a small table in the dining room. When it rang I would jump up on the chair, then on up on the table and root the receiver off the hook.

Someone would say "hello" and I'd say "hello". If it was a friend they would say, "Is that you, Priscilla?" About that time Mama would pick up the phone. Mama and her friends laughed and bragged on me. A pig answering the phone was considered a very clever trick.

If a stranger called, they'd hang up, thinking they had the wrong number. Sometimes they called back; sometimes they didn't.

I continued dreaming and resting until I heard the

car drive up and I knew it was morning.

Tom Cat was curled up next to my baby. They were both sound asleep. Some baby sitter he is!

I wanted to tell Mama and Papa right away about my baby, but I decided to act more dignified and let them discover her.

Quietly, I got up to eat, leaving my baby asleep on the straw.

Papa said good morning to me, checked my feed box and added more pellets. He brought fresh water and lettuce leaves from the super market.

Papa did not see my little girl. He really wasn't looking for a pig. And besides, she's quite tiny. But just as he stepped away from my pen, the little surprise woke up, and ushered forth a bunch of squeals that peeled the morning air.

Mama came through the barn door. She and Papa looked at each other.

"Where is that pig?" Papa asked.

The pig let out a couple more choice squeals. She wanted her mother. How could I deny her? By now it was obvious where "that pig" was.

Mama and Papa watched as I lay down with my baby. She was so grand. I was *proud* to show her off.

They were taken completely by surprise. Mama came in, loved my neck and cried. Papa cried too.

"Would you look at this, Papa? Our Priscilla has a pig! Oh, Priscilla," Mama blubbered, "Isn't she beautiful?"

Papa gently picked up the infant, gave it a loving pat and handed it to Mama. "It's a little girl," he said.

"Little Prissy," Mama announced, "You are a gorgeous, welcome surprise!"

"Should call her 'Copper', she's so rusty red," Papa said.

"You can call her anything you choose, but she will always be 'Little Prissy' to me."

"You were right, Porker," the Tom Cat said, looking on. "She's gonna call her Little Prissy. That's o.k. but I'm gonna call her Little Porker." He nodded a silly grin toward me and slithered out of the pen.

Chapter 24.

PROBLEMS

THIS day belongs to me and my baby. Little Prissy and I are getting acquainted, and I love it. I have no time for Hotsie, or T.C. or anyone else.

Sometimes, my little darling gets to be a big nuisance. When I want to step forward, she's in front of me. If I want to sit down, she's behind my sitter, if I have an itch, she's between me and my scratching place.

There's only one thing to do. Teach her some manners! After all, she is my responsibility. How she behaves is up to me.

Hotsie has been lying down all morning. I must have kept her awake last night. But I'm sure she won't mind if I ask her for some advice.

"Hotsie, are you awake?"

"Yes, Little One," she answered softly.

"I have a problem, Hotsie! You know I was raised by people and not by my mother. I know almost nothing about being a mother to a baby pig. I know only about being a people mother to a baby pig. I'm confused!"

"Would you listen to that?" An uncivil voice burst forth!

Oh! No! What is *she* doing back in the barn? My luck just ran out! Elsie is within ear-shot again!

With both front feet planted firmly on the top boards of her pen she delivered her spiteful oratory.

"Little Miss Super Pet is in trouble again! One lousy runt of a pig and she doesn't know what to do with it! Help her! Quick, somebody help her! Better yet, let the ugly dummy ask her *Mama.*"

Thank goodness Little Prissy was asleep! Being subjected to her Aunt Elsie's cruel behavior on the first day of her life, would pierce my heart! Oh! I wish there was a shot to give for hatefulness. I'd order up a double dose for Elsie, right away!

"Tomorrow, I'll be leaving this barn. I won't have to listen to *you* anymore, Elsie," Hattie said.

"That's tellin' her!" came a cheery voice from the rafters.

"Little Prissy has a fine mother. Pay no attention to Elsie. You, Little One, raise your infant as you see fit! Whatever is natural to you will be the right way." Hotsie's voice trailed off. I could barely hear her.

The dignity, not the volume, of Hotsie's voice always commanded attention. The most loved and respected sow in the barn, was my Hotsie. Even Elsie, would not dare talk back to Hotsie.

"I see nothing wrong with raising your baby *your* way, Priscilla. After all, you turned out beautifully." Hotsie added.

"Please don't talk anymore, Hotsie. Please! You are overtiring yourself. I treasure your advice and I shall be pleased to do as you have suggested," I told her.

I turned away from Hotsie, hoping she would rest. Anyway, it was time for Little Prissy's lunch, again!

As I lay there with my baby I thought upon Hotsie's words. They were, in fact, the words I had wanted to hear. I shall raise my baby as I was raised. To be kind, gentle, clean and to keep out of trouble.

Papa and Mama kept popping in. Little Prissy got used to them soon enough. Papa installed a heat lamp in one corner of my pen.

"Don't want that little thing to catch a chill, now do we, Priscilla?" he said. It wasn't likely. The weather had been quite nice.

Papa was switching sows around again. Several were moved, including Hattie. She'll be happy about the move. Of all the sows who dislike Elsie's behavior, Hattie is the most verbal about it.

Elsie stayed! For all I care he could have moved her to Cucamonga! Or one of those other places a long ways away. Maybe, if all went well, she would get lost on her way home!

I *know* that's not a nice way to talk about my sister! But Elsie is so aggravating, ------so rude. T.C. says she's *gross*. I think he means something like shamefully vulgar! And he's right!

Speaking of T.C., that sassy cat thinks he owns Little Prissy. He pops in all the time, giving out orders. "Be sure she gets enough to eat." "Don't let her fall in your drinking water." "Don't step on her." Etc. etc.

Everytime I turn around, there he is, wanting me to take a nap so he can baby sit! How many naps can I take in one day for gosh sakes? And besides! He can't be trusted as a baby sitter! When I go to sleep, so does he!

Papa had finished moving hogs. I hefted my front feet to the top boards of the pen to have a look around. From a standing position I could see a long way back. There was ol' Elsie, glaring, the way only Elsie can glare.

Victoria was across the hall again expecting another litter. Victoria was talking to herself. God only knows what she is cooking up!

So far the pen next to her is empty. Maybe Papa's gonna keep it that way!

There was Charlie, smiling back at me. "Hear you've been busy, Priscilla," he said cheerfully. "How are you getting along with your new family?"

"Gosh, Charlie, I like being called a family. But if a mother and one pig can be a family, then my family is doing just fine! How kind of you to ask! That one little pig has brought so much joy into my life," I told him.

On the other side of Hotsie a big old white sow was slowly getting up from her straw.

"Is that you over there, Mother?" I hollered.

"It's me, child! It's me! Congratulations! I want to hear all about it sometime. But now, we must not disturb our Hotsie. Last night was your night and tonight is hers," Mabel said.

One look confirmed Mabel's words. Hotsie had made her nest in the straw. She was resting and waiting.

"Hotsie! Please forgive me for neglecting you. How thoughtless of me! I'm so pre-occupied with myself and my baby that I failed to notice! Are you resting well, my friend?" I asked.

"Yes, Little One, and I am not the least bit offended. To see you so happy, warms my heart. I've rested all day. This is *not* my first litter, you know. But I *am* worried! Priscilla, I *must* have sixteen pigs. So *much* is expected of me! Once you set a high record there is no turning back. What would your Papa say if I came up with nine or ten pigs? He would be so disappointed." She shifted to a more comfortable position. "Enjoy your baby, Priscilla. Don't worry yourself needlessly about me. I'm an old hand at having babies!"

"My dear Hotsie," I began, "You have *nothing* to fear. Papa will be proud of you no matter how many pigs you have. After all, you've already given him one hundred and five pigs. *Who* could ask for more?" I had gotten her attention.

"Look at me!" I said. "*I'm* no big producer of pigs. Indeed I am the luckiest 'Porker' on the place. I have one little pig and I know I will never have another litter, but Mama and Papa haven't stopped

loving me and being proud of me. They know that
my misfortune was not of my own choosing."

"Well, well! Look who's giving advice!" Elsie in-
terupted, anxious to get in a few more quarrelsome
licks. "One lousy pig and she's an authority."

I had had *quite enough* of my sister and her *bad*
manners. I stood up so I could look her square in the
eye.

"Elsie," I said, in a loud, firm voice. Heads
turned! The sows were surprised! Elsie was caught off
guard!

"Perhaps I am not an authority on raising pigs!
And, I suppose I'm not even an authority on being
one myself! But I *am* an authority on Mama and Papa
----------wouldn't you say? *I know how they think.
They love every one of us!* Even you, Elsie!"

Tom Cat, always listening, came flying down
from the rafters, praising and applauding my action.

"You did it, Priscilla," he smiled radiantly! "You
stood up to her! You told her off!"

"Well ---if that's what 'telling off' is, then I did
it. I only meant to be firm with her. I'm tired to
death of her name calling," I confessed, knowing full
well that Elsie was listening to every word. "Mama
and Papa taught me to think for myself. Even if no
one agrees with me, *they* said I should be the best *me*
that I know how! It's too bad poor Elsie was raised
like a pig," I said, suddenly feeling quite sorry for

her.

"It's too bad poor Elsie was raised like a pig," Elsie mocked. "You creep! You idiot!" she shouted. "You think you're so smart! You don't talk like a pig! You don't walk like a pig! You don't even eat like a pig!"

"Thank goodness for *that*," I spouted back. "I don't want to be like *you*. That's for sure." I thought I was holding my own with her rather well. But arguing was not for me. I took no pleasure in it.

"Well you're not like me! *You are like nobody!* You've got one pig! *One* pig! -----And you can't even take care of *it*," Elsie blasted.

Her cruelty was too much for me. I could picture my little dead babies as she spoke, and Papa taking them away. I felt alone, sad and beaten.

T.C. begged me to "stick it to her" somemore. But I couldn't. I hated myself for exchanging unkind words with my sister. What had Elsie and I accomplished? Absolutely nothing!

Little Prissy had slept through the shouting. I was glad. Wouldn't have her think her mother was a nobody.

Gently, I lowered myself next to my daughter on the straw. She crept close to me, laid her head on my front leg and dropped off to sleep again.

How I loved her. Will she be like me? I wondered? Would that be so terrible? She won't be raised in the house as I was, but my peculiar manner is bound to influence her. Yet, most of my kind have accepted me, the way I am. All but Elsie, of course. If Elsie has sympathizers, they have not been vocal. Perhaps *she* is my only enemy.

Why do I care if she likes me or not? Ask me if I care! I *do* care. It pains my soul! Will I ever win her for a friend?

Chapter 25.

BABIES FOR HOTSIE

HOTSIE was busy! Very busy! Her pigs were anxious to be born. It was like someone had thrown open the starting gates at the race track!

Mama and Papa were in Hotsie's pen, watching and helping.

As soon as a pig is born and completely free from the mother, Mama picks it up and wipes it dry. Pigs are born with umbilical cords that are over a foot long. Papa ties a string around the cord, about two inches from the body, then cuts the cord with sterile sissors. The string stops the bleeding. Mama dabs the cut with some disinfectant, gives the pig a hug and places it on dry straw under the heat lamp.

When the pigs are dry and rested, Papa cuts their needle teeth. Or wolf teeth, whatever you want to to call them. At any rate the tips of those sharp little

black fangs should be removed. Else they can injure
the sow's nipples. And nobody wants that, the pigs or
the sow! All eight of the teeth, four above and four
below, are clipped with a pair of wire cutters. The
pigs squeal, but they aren't hurt a bit. It's painless.

Mitzi was watching. The Tom Cat was not
around.

Little Prissy and I lay on our straw and peeked
through the fence. It was exciting! All those healthy
pigs being born so fast. Lucky Hotsie!

This blessed event provoked a steady stream of
questions from Little Prissy.

"Mama, may I go over and see the new pigs next
door?" she asked.

"No, my precious. Not yet. You must wait until
all of them are born," I cautioned.

"I can crawl through the boards in the fence," she
continued.

"I know you can, you are very strong. But you
must not! Not yet!" I told her.

"How come Hotsie is white and you are red and
white, Mama?" she asked, never taking her eyes off
Hotsie.

"It's a matter of breed. Hotsie is a pure bred
Chester White. My mother was a white Landrace and
my father was a black and white Hampshire."

"But Mama, I don't understand. If your mother
was white and your father was black and white, how

come you aren't black and white?" She made me
laugh, but I could see she was quite clever. "And how
come," she continued, "you have a pretty white belt
around your middle and I don't?" So much to learn.
She was filled with curiosity. Her adoring brown eyes
searched my face for answers.

"A little pig inherits color not only from its parents but from its grandparents as well. Your grandfather, Nebraska, was red. Papa called him 'Big Red'.
You look a lot like him, Prissy. Sometimes, every pig
in a litter will be a different color," I told her.

"What colors were my brothers and sisters,
Mama?" she asked sadly. "Were some like you?"

"Yes. Some were like me, but let's talk about
something else," I suggested. "Peek through the
fence. Count Hotsie's babies." That would give her
something to do and at the same time she could
practice her counting.

My old friend was completely surrounded by pigs.
One was sleeping across her nose. A tiny white one
was being shoved away from a choice eating place.
The one doing the shoving was a big red one with a
white spot on its rump. An ornery boy, no doubt.

"One, two, three, four ----five, seven --"

"Six," I corrected her.

"Six, seven, nine --"

"Eight," I corrected.

"Eight, nine, ten, eleven ---there's eleven, Mama,"

she said sweetly.

"How many pigs are there with white belts?"

"One, two, three, four, five, seven --"

"Six," I again corrected.

"There are six. I don't want to count anymore now, Mama. I'm sleepy."

Was she really sleepy or was she just tired of school? No matter. I let her have her way. I love her so. She's pure delight to me.

"Go ahead, Little Prissy. Take a nap. When you are finished sleeping Hotsie will have lots more babies to count." I said.

"More than eleven?" she asked sleepily.

"Maybe as many as *sixteen*!" I was hopeful.

As soon as she closed her eyes, the Tom Cat appeared out of nowhere! He crept over by Little Prissy and curled himself up for a snooze. That cat!

I turned my attention to Hotsie's pen. "The pigs are coming too far apart now to suit me," Papa said. "She's a few days early! A few days can make a difference. Hotsie seems to be quite comfortable though." He sounded troubled!

"Don't worry dear, it's her eighth litter. She has a perfectly good right to slow down a little," Mama said. "Only we women folk know about having babies! Isn't that right, Priscilla?" she asked, when she noticed I was listening.

"That's right, Mama," I agreed.

"I swear! The way you two carry on beats me!" Papa scratched his head and squinted and eye toward Mama. "Are you just puttin' me on, or can you and that little pet of yours really understand each other?"

"She takes it for granted that we understand her language because she understands ours! Priscilla is intelligent! I'm surprised you can't understand her!" Mama said. "Experts are saying now that pigs at birth function as well as a two year old child. Little Prissy is bound to be exceptional! She's already helping Priscilla spruce up the place. And of course she talked and walked the minute she was born like an ordinary pig. But with Priscilla to teach her, yes, she's bound to be exceptional!" Mama turned and looked at Papa. A heavyhearted look! She was worried about something. "Papa, you must promise me one thing."

"A promise?" he asked. "What if I couldn't keep it?"

"I know you love Priscilla, perhaps as much as I do and you would never consider selling her. Now I must ask you, please Papa, please don't ever sell Little Prissy either." Mama begged.

Sell my baby? The thought had not occurred to me! I listened and prayed.

Papa was sitting on an overturned bucket. He got up and looked into my pen. My heart thumped and throbbed! I tried to read the answer in his face. How could he sell my baby? How could he?

Papa sells pigs all the time! They are sold to other farmers for breeding stock. The *other* sows don't seem to mind! But the *other* sows have lots of pigs! Little Prissy is my only child. I will never have more babies! The vet said so!

Papa reached for the brush. I wasn't sure I wanted him to touch me! He stepped over the fence, into my pen and began to brush my back. Meanwhile, Mama and I waited anxiously for an answer. Papa took his own sweet time.

"This pig has all the makings for a good brood sow. She's healthy enough. I'll have to admit, Mama, your Priscilla is a terrific mother. The way she cleans this pig's face is something most unusual! Bet it's the first pig that ever got its face licked clean after each lunch."

"She picked that habit up in the house from the dog and cat," Mama said. "Priscilla has always liked to be clean. Remember how she used to root at a napkin in the palm of my hand to clean her face?"

"Yes. And I remember something else about Priscilla and napkins. The time that baby chicken jumped out of its box in the house. Priscilla ran and stuffed Mitzi's drinking water full of napkins," Papa said.

"So the chicken wouldn't fall in and drown!" Mama added proudly.

I liked that little chicken. Mitzi and I jumped in its box a couple of times. Cleo would fly up on one of our backs and we'd all take a nap.

"I know Priscilla is smart, but poking napkins in the drinking water to keep a chicken from drowning? Mama! That's a little far fetched," Papa chuckled. "It is ridiculous! But if that pig is as smart as you say she is, well, maybe it's true after all."

Mama propped her hands on her hips and stood up to Papa. "Priscilla is the smartest hog that ever lived!"

"Whatever you say, Mama," Papa grinned. "I know how much you love your Priscilla. You know I could *never* sell Little Prissy. Priscilla is like part of our family and I suppose her Little Prissy will be the same way. We'll not sell it, Mama. We'll just keep her with her mother."

Boy! What a relief! It sure took him long enough to say it. I didn't think he'd sell her, but it sure was good to hear him say so!

Mama hugged Papa's neck.

He hugged her back.

I'm surprised Mama asked Papa about selling Little Prissy, in front of me. And besides, Mama would never have let him sell her anyway. Now that I think about it, I should have known I had nothing to worry about.

While all this was going on, Hotsie had only one more pig. A total now of twelve.

There were tears in Hotsie's eyes. Without asking,

I know what's on her mind. Papa!

I can almost read her thoughts: "He's so good to me. He calls me his queen and loves to brag on me to all his friends. I must never have less than sixteen pigs in a litter." That's what she's thinking!

The people 50% of me says, "Tell Mama about the tear in Hotsie's eye. And why it's there!"

But my 50% hog sense tells me not to. Hotsie would not approve.

The hour grew late. No more pigs were born. Papa and Mama left for the house.

"Reckon she's all done," Papa had said. He gave Hotsie a gentle pat, glanced lovingly at the pigs and they were gone for the night.

Hotsie was busy. With twelve kids, who wouldn't be busy?

I got up and leaned over the top boards of my pen, "Your babies are lovely! Congratulations!"

"There will be more," she said quickly, as if apologizing.

Poor Hotsie! It's pure and simple, she can't accept the truth! Only twelve pigs!

Strange! She's unhappy with twelve, while I'm so delighted with just one. But, I've never set a record. Papa will never call me a "queen". At least Mama says I'm bright and kind. That's something! And they both think I'm a good mother!

Perhaps I should try to reassure Hotsie. "You'll have other big litters, my friend!"

"No, there will be more babies tonight!" she insisted.

"You've had them all, Hotsie! Do you think Papa would have gone to the house if you were going to have more pigs? You know he wouldn't!"

Hotsie began to cry. "It's different this time, Little One. My pigs are slower in coming. Something is wrong! I don't know just what. Perhaps, I gained too much weight. I don't know. I feel strange! The Mr. *thought* I was through having pigs, but there will be more."

"Why don't you rest with your babies, Hotsie?" She did not answer.

Chapter 26.

A PAINFUL LOSS

I N the night I was awakened by a cry of great pain! It startled me! I sprang to my feet to investigate! Was it Hotsie?

"Hotsie, are you awake?" I whispered. "I can't see you very well! How do you feel?"

"I feel awful," Hotsie answered, gasping for breath! "I should be warm, but I'm cold! And I'm shaking so! Disturbing my babies!"

"Don't fret yourself! A bad case of nerves, that's your problem! Needless worry has made you ill!" My eyes became more accustomed to the dark. "What do I have to say to convince you? Papa will be satisfied with you! You'll see! Why, look at me! One baby, and they still love me!" I told her.

"I'm going to have more pigs tonight," she persisted.

"Stop torturing yourself! Put it out of your mind

186

and go to sleep. You need rest!"

"I'm afraid, Priscilla," Hotsie cried, "I feel like my whole body is coming apart!"

Afraid? Hotsie was *no* coward! *Something is dreadfully wrong!* Her *pain* is real! Far beyond a case of nerves, as I had supposed.

I wished for Papa and Mama. Oh, how I wished for them! But morning was still several hours away. They suspected no problem. The newborns were fine, but Hotsie, if Papa was here right now, he'd call Dr. Pearson!

Hotsie panted, groaned and shook violently! I could not bear to see her suffer so!

"Priscilla," she whispered. "Is there a God who takes care of us after we die?"

"Sure Hotsie! Mama and Papa told me so. Sometime, when you're feeling better, we can talk about it."

"There will be no other time for me," she cried.

"No! No! Hotsie, please -----don't even think a horrible thing like that! Think of your babies! What would they do without you?"

She became very quiet.

I felt helpless! Was it true? Was she dying? I could not stand it! The very thought of it made me quake!

"Hotsie," I called to her. There was no answer.

"Hotsie!" I called in a loud voice! Still no answer!

"Hotsie! Hotsie!" I screamed. "Say something to

me! Let me know! I must know! Are you all right?"
Silence.

I was terrified of the possible truth! I had to
know!

I raced around and around my pen telling myself
I could jump the fence that divided our pens! Little
Prissy ran to a corner, seeking safety! I can do it! I
told myself I could, but the fence was high -----really
high! I had to get to her and there was no other way!
I could wait no longer! I said a prayer and thrust myself up and over! Somehow, I managed to clear the
fence, with inches to spare!

Hotsie was dead! There were four more babies, all
born dead. She had been right all along. There *were*
more pigs, sixteen in all. She had matched her record,
but had lost her life.

Her body was still and cold. The newborn babes
were huddled together by her head. Some were
asleep. But some had no doubt witnessed their mother's suffering and her death. How dreadful!

I was stunned! Hotsie dead! Unbelievable!

For a long time, I just stood there, and wept!

Dawn was not far off. Mama and Papa would
come, but it was no use. Hotsie, was gone.

Little Prissy heard my sobs. "What's the matter,
Mama?" she asked, poking her head through the
fence. Once again her little eyes were full of questions
when she saw the horrid sight.

"Our friend Hotsie is dead. We must be very brave. There is work to do here. We must look after these babies. If it were me lying there dead, Hotsie would look after you." I sobbed.

"But Mama! There are so many of them." She looked surprised!

"We can make do! Now see if you can squeeze through the fence," I instructed.

Little Prissy stuck her right front leg and then her left one through the boards. She squeezed herself forward, a little at a time.

"I'm stuck," she announced. "I can't get through and I can't back up."

Sure enough. She looked like a teeter-totter. First

her head bobbed up and then her tail.

T.C. jumped down from the rafters. He licked Little Prissy around the middle until she was slick. Then he gave her a shove. Plop! She fell in.

"You are clever indeed, Tom Cat," I said.

"Of course," he answered. But there was no silliness about his manner this night, for he too loved Hotsie.

When I had scooted the four lifeless little bodies close to their mother, I covered them, as best I could, with straw. I worked and cried.

Then I made another straw bed near Hotsie and lay down with Little Prissy.

One by one, twelve sad little orphans made their way to me, for the warmth of my body and a place to satisfy their hunger.

"We'll make do, Mama," Little Prissy whispered to me, just before she fell asleep. "We'll make do."

Yes, but what about Papa?

His Hotsie, gone!

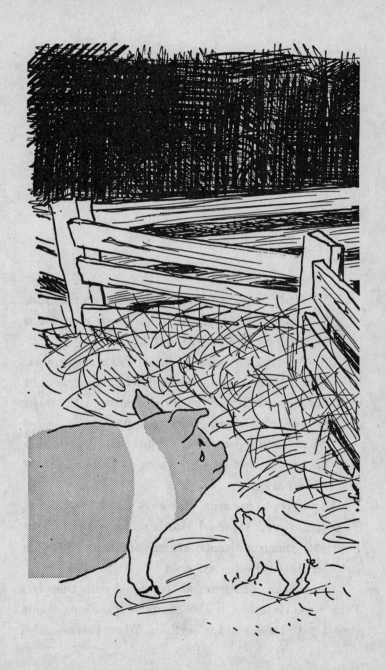

Chapter 27.

FAMILY AND FAME

WHEN I reached the state of utter exhaustion, I slept. But not for long. Dawn closed the door on an unholy night.

If only I could have prepared Papa and Mama. They stood there now, in total shock! Papa stared in disbelief. First at Hotsie, covered scantily with straw. And then at me. His sober face grew pale.

"What has happened here?" he cried. Papa took a step backward as if he were going to faint. He grabbed hold of my gate.

Mama took his arm. Her eyes filled with tears! Together, they examined Hotsie's body for clues to her death. Such a disappointment for Papa to see his beloved Hotsie lifeless and cold.

Mama was not surprised to see me with the pigs. Papa was. He asked me all kinds of questions about how I got in there and everything. When I answered---

192

he didn't listen. Mama listened, and understood.

"Who else but Priscilla would jump a five foot fence ----in the dead of night ----to take on another sow's pigs? Twelve of them at that!" Mama looked at me lying on the floor nursing thirteen pigs. "It appears Priscilla has adopted the whole family! What a girl! Had it not been for her bravery, they might all be dead this morning!"

"I've never heard of such a thing! As long as I've been raisin' hogs! I've never heard of such a thing! A sow jumpin' a high fence like this one, to mother another sow's pigs! This is one for the books!" he managed a smile. "She *is* brave Mama, and the most unselfish hog I have ever seen."

His praise made me feel foolish, for I did not feel brave! I felt --love for Hotsie and her children and I feel ---responsible! That's what I feel. Because Hotsie was my friend I feel responsible to carry on for her.

Papa is always saying that friends should help each other.

"As soon as I finish the chores, I'll take out that center fence. Priscilla has two litters. She's entitled to two pens!"

How about that! He referred to my *one* pig as a litter! That was nice of Papa.

Although he was talking about *me* he never took his eyes off of his dead sow. There were still tears in his eyes, and in Mama's.

"She'll be too heavy for us to pull out of the pen, Mama," he said about Hotsie. "I'll call Roy Hill and have him come with a couple of his boys. Getting her out of there will be a real chore. She weighs at least eight hundred pounds!"

Mama stayed with me. She knelt down to check out each little pig ------its color, sex, eyes, ears, nose and tail. Then, one by one, she gave them a big kiss and a greeting to the world. Little Prissy got picked up and kissed in between all the others. Wasn't hard to figure! Mama is partial to *my* baby. Little Prissy loved all the attention.

"You've taken on a lot of extra work, Priscilla," Mama said. "But if anybody deserves a family, you do! You were cheated out of a family when you were growing up and almost cheated out of having a family of your own. I hope Little Prissy doesn't mind sharing you with Hotsie's children!"

"No, she doesn't mind. She agreed with me that we can make do. I'm so proud of her," I told Mama. "She isn't a bit selfish. You and Papa would have been proud of Hotsie too! She was miserable, fighting for her life and in great pain but so-o courageous. I didn't know she was dying, Mama." She hugged my neck. "And I didn't even tell her good-bye!" I cried. "We *will* see Hotsie again someday, when we die -------- won't we?"

"I'm sure we will, Priscilla. Now don't you worry

about Hotsie. She'll be just fine. ------Right now, we've got plenty to do. You and the pigs will have to go back to *your* pen so Papa and I can clean and disinfect this one. This time, you won't have to jump over. We'll use the gates!"

About an hour later Hotsie and her four little dead babies were taken out. I couldn't look!

When the pens had been cleaned and fresh shavings and straw added, Papa took out the center fence as promised.

My life had suddenly, dramatically changed. Yesterday, I had one little pig and thoughts of my dead babies. Today, I have thirteen babies, thoughts of my dead children and of Hotsie and the tragedy we shared on the last night of her life.

Life is strange! Perhaps I should be thankful for the sorrow to make me appreciate the joy, but I am not.

T.C. had not been far away. He bore his grief in silence, high in the rafters. A peculiar cat our T.C., many sides to his character. He is a friend to be counted on, but he's horribly nosy -----misses nothing! Once in a while he crawls in under the heat lamps with the pigs. When the pigs get too rough, snuggling up next to his fur, he creeps up on the back of the sleeping mother. When the pigs settle back down to sleep, he very quietly maneuvers his way down with them again.

He spends more time with me and in the rafters above my pen than anywhere else, unless he's love-making! If a couple of days passed without seeing him, I knew he was chasing one of his female friends. All female cats hold him in high regard. He told me so himself!

Mitzi hasn't been around lately. Mama said it was because she has puppies in the house.

The barn was quiet. How odd! The gossip and grumbling I'd gotten used to is missing today. Even Elsie was quiet! That *was* strange! I *do* believe I heard Elsie cry when Hotsie died! Could it be that Elsie has a heart, after all?

Tom Cat dropped by. "You are something of a female type hero today, Priscilla, a ------Florence Nightingale!"

"Me?" I asked.

"That's what I'm hearing, all over the place, Porker!" he answered. "Your family grew, I see!" The pigs were all under the heat lamp and I was getting a much needed rest!

"One of mine and twelve of Hotsie's. She had six-teen in all, you know." I wanted to be sure everyone knew the number.

"What are they saying about me, T.C.?" I asked.

"It was what you did for Hotsie! You probably think nobody paid any attention to what you were doing last night. Right? Well ----wrong. Every hog in the place was awake! None of them would have done what you did, Porker! Play leap-frog with a five foot fence? Never! Not unless they wanted to get out of the barn, or start a fight! Sows don't care for each other's pigs! In fact, they'd soon trample them to death! But here *you* are. Different! You showed them what 'kindness' is. Today, you look 'majestic' to them. Hotsie is gone and now they have another to look up to and to revere. You, Priscilla! You have become their idol!" Tom Cat seemed sincere enough. I do hope he's not making this up. Yet, I was somewhat disturbed by what he said.

I want the sows to like me, but I don't want to take Hotsie's place -----only as a mother to her babies, for now.

I am not majestic! "Hotsie" was majestic! I don't want to be an idol, though I did idolize Hotsie!

"If the sows admire me because of my kindness, then ----well -----that's good! Being mean makes a person ugly and sick, works the same way for a hog! I'm surprised that Elsie isn't sick all the time!" I said.

"Hold on, Priscilla," T.C. blurted. "I think you might be in for a surprise at her change in heart!"

"Change of heart? Elsie? She'll never change! She hates me and takes pure delight in heckling me!"

"You'll see!" The Tom Cat had that *I know something you don't* look on his face, again. He then slithered through the boards and was gone.

As the days went by, no two were the same. The pigs ate and slept, and slept and ate. And grew! Keeping them clean, kept me busy. I licked their faces clean and rubbed them dry with straw. Mama told me I didn't have to do that. Other sows don't, she said. But then, I never was like the other sows. I'm just me. So I continued to clean 'em up.

I wonder what T.C. meant about Elsie?

Chapter 28.

CHANGES

WHEN Hotsie's pigs were five weeks old, Papa moved them to the feeder barn. As much as I loved the little fellows I never claimed them. They were Hotsie's. I raised the pigs ----but I did it for her.

Once the pigs were gone it *was* more peaceful. They had gotten so big that when they nursed, they scooted me clear across the pen!

Little Prissy got to stay with me. The way she porked down her pellets, it was time to wean her too. Although she complained, I stuck with it. Sometimes, I had to sleep on my belly to keep her from snitching!

Since Dr. Pearson told Mama and Papa not to breed me again, they never did. I was kept for a pet and felt extremely privileged.

Little Prissy grew up fast! Too fast to suit me! I

remember when Mama wished for a shot to keep me small so I could live in the house. Now *I'm* wishing for such a shot! For my Prissy.

My baby has turned into a real beauty. She's good natured and gentle. Papa left her in my pen until she was expecting her first litter. Then she was moved next door. To Hotsie's old pen.

Mabel just moved out from across the hall after weaning another litter of thirteen pigs. She's getting up in years, my mother, but she has lost the limp and the pain that went with it. Papa found out about putting apple cider vinegar in her drinking water. It cured the arthritis in her joints, a problem that had plagued her since she was so badly bitten.

When Mabel moved out --Elsie moved in!

Since the night of Hotsie's tragic death, Elsie has been almost civilized! Tom Cat said I'd see a great change in her! Seeing it with my own eyes would be *almost* believing!

Elsie was eyeing Little Prissy's new home.

"I want that pen!" she announced.

"How do you intend getting it?" Little Prissy snapped.

"Don't worry about it," she answered sharply. "I'll get it!"

So, she's changed huh? Doesn't sound like it to me! But, I'm willing to give her a chance. After all, she *is* my sister!

"Am I to understand that you want the pen next to me?" I asked her sternly.

"Quite right! And I intend to have it." Elsie demanded. "Are you surprised 'sister'?"

"Of course! This sudden desire of yours to be my neighbor -----. Yes, I *am* surprised! Very surprised! Never once have you shown an inclination to be near *me*!" I said.

"I have my reasons," Elsie spouted. She turned away, fluffed up her straw and lay down.

Little Prissy and I discussed the matter. My Prissy was afraid we would be separated. I was not. And I set about to convince her. I know Mama! Allow us to be separated? Never!

One thing constantly bothered me while Prissy was growing up. *Would she be a social outcast among her peers?*

I raised her peculiarly, I know! But here she is ----- all grown up, well adjusted, and treated kindly, by the sows. She's independent of me, though, and has a bit of a temper!

Why did Elsie want Prissy's pen? I glanced about and up above my head for T.C. When it comes to tracking down information, Tom Cat is the greatest! *Now* I had a need for his talent.

I spied the cat lying on a wooden barrel just outside the barn door, sunning himself.

"Psst -----Tom Cat!" I extended my voice to be

heard by him and not by Elsie. Immediately, I had his attention. He started toward me, waddling sleepily from side to side.

"You called?" he asked, toying with me.

"Tom Cat I need some information." He came closer. I had whetted his appetite. His sleepy expression shot straight ahead to eagerness. He cocked an ear sideways to my mouth.

"Go on," he grinned. "Go on, go on!"

"It's about Elsie," I began.

Tom Cat's face lit up! His eyes clicked from side to side! "Aw haw! You want to get even with the old rip! I never thought I'd see the day!"

"Sorry to break your bubble, dear heart, but it's nothing as revolting as that. I don't want to start a war! You see ----Elsie wants to move next door! Have you heard? She's demanding Prissy's pen! I know she will never get *that* pen, but why, why does she want it? It seems to be very important to her!"

"Hmmm ------strange indeed!" the Tom Cat said, casting a suspicious glance toward Elsie.

At the moment Elsie looked perfectly harmless. She snored with loud gusts. With each puff she blew more cedar shavings from the floor. Soon, she had cleared a large spot by her nose.

T.C. and I both laughed.

"Never fear! T.C. is here! I shall scout around, listen and look!" he was showing off. "When I finish you will have a book." He had made a rhyme and he knew it.

"I know I will!" I laughed as he sprang to the top boards, and was gone.

His ability to ferret out information is a work of art. He sits quietly in the rafters, listening! More than once I've seen a sow glance above her head before she shared a bit of gossip. Was *he* up there? And now, his special talent would come in handy.

My hip itched! I looked for a place to scratch it. So many good, rough, rubbing spots had worn smooth. I tried the gate post again, remembering a spot on the lower half that was yet quite sufficient. Getting down low enough to scratch the itch, was a problem. It isn't easy to maneuver a four hundred pound body.

Itching was not my only problem. Sometimes I had no taste for food at all. A peculiar situation for a hog. I'm expected to eat!

Papa tries his best to perk up my appetite. A variety of food keeps coming. One day he brought the most beautiful apples I have ever seen. I ate three. Little Prissy ate a bucket full and wanted more. There is no doubt about her appetite. She makes a real pig of herself!

Papa brings sweet corn, green beans, squash, watermelon, grapes and lettuce. Mama says when he walks through the garden he looks for something to tempt me. One day he brought me cabbage! I hate cabbage!

I try my best to eat some of everything, not wanting to be troublesome. Papa always returns to pick up what I've left ------before it spoils. Although Little Prissy bids me eat, she wastes no time in enjoying my leftovers.

I know something is wrong with me! But I don't know what it is!

Chapter 29.

LIFE AND DEATH

DR. Pearson came today to patch up another one of Lulu-bell's victims. The sows should have more sense than to mess around with her. Lulu-bell can really inflict pain when she loses her temper. She bites hard and rips the flesh. Papa keeps her though. She's a good mother.

While Dr. Pearson was there Mama asked him to have a look at me. She filled him in on my condition, my poor appetite and reminded him that I was the sow that lost the entire litter, save one.

The doctor gave me a shot in the rump. I hated it! He used a lot of big words to discribe my illness. It had something to do with being lain on by my mother when I was a baby.

The purpose of the shot was to make me hungry. It worked for a few days. Then food began to make me sick! So I ate even less.

Mama spent more and more time in my pen. She knew I needed her. Life has played some cruel tricks on me, but whatever the crisis, Mama was there.

When a sow has a new litter I can't help being envious. There will be no more babies for me. I've been the only mother I will ever be. I'm done for, as a producer of pigs, forever.

Every now and then Mama and Papa put a pig in my pen to keep me company. I always sense the pig's dislike for me! Just as I did Prissy and Hotise's pigs, I lick them clean and rub them dry with a mouthful of straw. The little visitors aren't used to me. They don't like me much, as a baby sitter. Never the less I enjoy the company of the little critters.

T.C. came to call wearing his famous *I know something you don't* grin.

"Have I got news for you!" he whispered.

"What about?" I asked.

"Elsie!" he answered. "Elsie told Charlie. Charlie told Blossom. Blossom told Rachel. Rachel told Victoria. Victoria says 'hello' and, Victoria told me why Elsie wants to be your neighbor." The silly grin he was wearing made me even more curious.

"I knew I could count on you. Don't keep me waiting! Tell me ------why?"

"Elsie would never tell *you* this, Porker, she's too darn stubborn! Victoria says Elsie brags on you to everybody! She chatters on and on about your bravery, about your compassion for Hotsie and your dutiful service to Hotsie's children," T.C. related.

"Tom Cat, do you know what this means?" I cried. "My sister likes me!"

"Likes you? She adores you, Porker! Even if she doesn't show it, you are the apple of her eye, the sister of her choice. Her jealousy has turned to pure admiration and fond affection." The Tom Cat drew out each word as if he were tasting the sweetness of it.

"There's more," he continued. "Elsie has this notion about feeling safe next to you. She saw how you came to Hotsie's rescue. Do you get it, Priscilla? Do you understand why she wants Hotsie's old pen? Some nerve! How could she possibly think you would do the same for her? Since the day you arrived in the farrowing barn, Elsie has caused you nothing but trouble!"

I wanted to tell Tom Cat he was wrong about me. Yes, I *would* help Elsie, if she needed help. She's my sister. But I couldn't tell him. All I could do was cry tears of joy!

To think, Elsie likes me! She was the first and the last to make fun of my "people personality". Now I feel complete, fulfilled.

"Thank you for bringing me word, my friend," I managed to say. "Remember how frightened I was to move to the farrowing barn? I just knew I would never fit in. And now," I cried, "with Elsie's change of heart ------I think it's safe to say, I have no known enemies!"

"You are some kind of a great lady, Priscilla. Too bad you're not a cat!" He smiled and slithered away through the fence.

As the days passed, Little Prissy grew larger, round and lovely, while I grew weaker each day. Dr. Pearson visited me often. He had done all he could do for me.

I realized I would soon die. Wherever my friend Hotsie and our dead babies had gone, perhaps I would go there too.

One day when Mama and Papa were cleaning my pen, I told Mama about Elsie's great desire to be my neighbor. I knew that Mama would never separate me from Little Prissy, so I asked for the next best thing.

"Mama," I asked. "When my pen becomes empty would you please put Elsie in it." With tears in her eyes, she promised.

The end is near for me. And now she knows that I know.

A few nights later while Mama and Papa delivered Little Prissy's first litter, I fluffed up my straw for the last time. Friend Tom Cat watched from his perch, high in the rafters.

"Little Prissy ----your babies are lovely," I whispered through the fence. I did not want to be troublesome.

"One little girl looks just like you, Mother," she replied. "Mama has already named her Patsy.

"I hope I can be a good mother. I want to be just like you. You are the greatest mother in the whole world!"

What a joy Little Prissy had been to me.

"Oh my Prissy," I replied softly, "without you my life would have had no meaning. You are the fulfillment of my dreams! The family I almost never had. You are my miracle! I do love you so!"

"And I love you, Mother," she said sweetly.

Slowly, I lowered my weary body to the straw. Life ---------was leaving me.

I heard Elsie say, "I love you, my brave sister." Though her words thrilled my soul, I could not answer.

I closed my eyes for the last time! And when I did I saw a delightful sight! A lovely white sow moved gracefully toward me. She was not alone.

Could it be?

With her were thirteen little pigs. I recognized them all.

Four I had once covered with straw!

And the rest? Well, they were mine!

"Hello, Little One," she said happily. "Welcome! Come, see my fine apple orchard."

The End